TIPS AND TRICKS FOR STRESS-FREE TRAVEL

NANZIE

INDIA • SINGAPORE • MALAYSIA

ISBN 979-8-89322-839-7

I am grateful to the practice of Nichren Buddhism and our eternal mentor Dr. Daisaku Ikeda for continuously encouraging us through his life and words. This practice has taught me that there is nothing that cannot be achieved and we all have infinite potential to pursue all our dreams.

It is God's wish that you must explore his creation. God created a world full of magical places to be explored for us to be immersed in its magic and beauty. So let us indulge, dig and savor the exquisite creation of the almighty.

In the memory of Shirley and Stuffy.

I dedicate this book to myself as a gift of year 2017 and my passion to remain positive in all phases of life.

I travel to celebrate

I travel to forget

I travel to evolve

I travel to make things better

I travel to make life worthwhile

Contents

Acknowledgements

I would like to thank everyone who helped me make this book a reality.

With deep respect and great love for Reema Khanna, philosopher, pillar of strength and inspiration. One who has lifted my spirits in all phases of life and introduced me to the newfound talent of writing a book. You're like a guiding lighthouse for me, a beacon of light that not only shines brightly but also provides unwavering guidance, helping to find our way and stay on the right path amidst life's uncertainties.

Special thanks to Amanpreet Chaddha a homemaker, for her constant support and encouragement. I'm grateful for your friendship and I deeply appreciate your support during thick and thin, sometimes just offering hug I needed at the end of the day is a source of immense comfort and strength.

Heartfelt thanks to Priyanka Malhotra for her insights on chapters 1–4 and 8, and to Bhumija Batra for her valuable suggestions regarding the cover page.

Love and Hugs to Suhaan Khanna for his creative ideas.

I am indebted to Mr. Anil Anand; Air France/ KLM Regional Station Manager at that time; for his positive, inspirational, and forward-thinking approach to various situations. His leadership style fosters a culture of innovation and collaboration, inspiring everyone to reach their full potential. Moreover, his dedication to excellence and commitment to customer satisfaction set a high standard for us all to follow. His mentorship has not only helped me grow professionally but has also instilled in me a sense of confidence and determination to tackle any challenge head-on.

With that I hope you are ready to stroll - Globe Trails.

Feeling my way through the darkness
Guided by a beating heart
I can't tell where the journey will end
But I know where to start
They tell me I'm too young to understand
They say I'm caught up in a dream
Well life will pass me by if I don't open up my eyes
Well that's fine by me
So wake me up when it's all over
When I'm wiser and I'm older
All this time I was finding myself, and I
Didn't know I was lost
So wake me up when it's all over
When I'm wiser and I'm older
All this time I was finding myself, and I
Didn't know I was lost
I tried carrying the weight of the world
But I only have two hands
Hope I get the chance to travel the world
But I don't have any plans
Wish that I could stay forever this young
Not afraid to close my eyes
Life's a game made for everyone
And love is a prize
So wake me up when it's all over
When I'm wiser and I'm older
All this time I was finding myself, and I
Didn't know I was lost
So wake me up when it's all over
When I'm wiser and I'm older
All this time I was finding myself, and I
I didn't know I was lost
Wake me up - by Avicii

Prologue

Embark on a European adventure with three friends. A trip meant for thrill turns into a journey of unexpected challenges when two lose their passports. Join them as they navigate the highs and lows of foreign travel from the very start.

We travel to make sure we don't miss out life's adventure and experiences.

Chapter 1

Preparing for departure: Booking, accommodation, and transportation.

Traveling with friends to Europe, where the husband is a senior citizen and the wife, my friend, is over 55, was an interesting experience. Despite the age gap, I couldn't figure out if they chose to travel with me for safety reasons or simply to enjoy the trip in a group.

As friends, Annie proposed a trip to Europe, and I, Rebecca, always excited about international adventures, wholeheartedly agreed. Alongside Annie's husband, Peter, we organized our European journey and concluded that an Asian airline offered the most budget-friendly option in our travel planning.

Oddly, Peter urged me to make the booking first, assuring that they would secure their tickets later. Occasionally, I wondered if my friends, Annie and her husband Peter, being senior citizens, were perhaps worried about me backing out of the trip. This could explain their insistence on me booking first. Nevertheless, I assured them of my commitment to the trip and explained the necessity of booking through my preferred websites, vendors, and airline due to the miles I could accumulate. Given my aviation experience, I had specific airline preferences, including KLM, Air France, United, Cathay Pacific, and Air India. Moreover, I prefer non-stop flights lasting approximately 8 hours over connecting flights, that result in a total travel time of 12-15 hours to Europe. I feel that opting for non-stop flights may not be the preference of those seeking more economical choices. Therefore, I advised Annie to proceed with their flight bookings, preventing any potential blame for the delay in my booking that might have led to increased ticket prices for them.

Tip: While purchasing ticket:

1. Lowest-priced tickets are Tuesday & Wednesday due to lower demand and fewer travellers.
2. Most economical days to fly out - Tuesday, Wednesday, and Saturday.
3. Ticket prices can vary depending on various factors such as destination, time of year, airline promotions, and market fluctuations.

When seeking budget-friendly flights, one of my preferred strategies is consulting travel agents for vacation packages, which provides insights into 3–4-star hotels and local activities. This approach allows me to compare the best booking options, either online or through a travel agency, without committing to a package. The itinerary provided by the travel agent offers insight on the timing and duration of activities, as well as the main attractions. This not only saves me time on research but also helps me plan and book activities once I reach the destination country.

Tip: Ask a travel agent for a package deal. This lets you refer to the activities listed in the package and explore them independently in the destination country.

Annie purchased budget-friendly flight tickets at an affordable price, which included a layover in Asia and a total travel time of 14 hours, allowing for one checked baggage. Conversely, in my case, I conducted thorough research to secure the best deal for my tickets. This involved considering factors such as credit card rewards, weekend promotions, non-stop flights, absence of transit visa requirements, shorter travel times with connections, and airlines that could increase my existing mileage balance. Eventually, I secured a direct flight from Delhi to Paris with my preferred airline, inclusive of two checked bags, and a flight duration of 9 hours. The convenience of having two checked bags is valuable, as it eliminates concerns about weight restrictions due to shopping. Moreover, having a two-bag allowance streamlines the check-in procedure for carry-on luggage when traveling with just one suitcase, enabling the option to check in hand luggage for a hands-free experience.

Tip: Opt for booking nonstop flights whenever possible. While you may find irresistible deals with multiple layovers, picking a non-stop flight can really cut down on any extra trouble and inconvenience.

Tip: Different credit cards offer promotions where you can earn extra points for purchasing airline tickets or receive discounts.

Tip: Booking flights with an airline or its partner airlines will increase the miles on your existing mileage card. Accumulating miles can lead to earning free tickets to various destinations.

Tip: If prioritizing cost savings, consider booking a ticket with 1-2 layovers, even though this might result in a loss of one day during the journey.

Tip: If prioritizing time and comfort, opt for a non-stop flight. This choice will save you a day of travel.

Annie expressed a desire to make the remaining reservations together. I agreed but clarified that expenses in Euros would be settled in Euros, and expenses in INR would be in INR.

Our flight routes differed: Annie and Peter's itinerary took them from Delhi to Dubai to Brussels, while mine had a direct route to Paris. Despite the difference in our flight routes, our intention was to meet up in Brussels. Upon learning that I was scheduled to arrive in Paris at 8:00 PM and they would reach Brussels at 10:00 AM the next day, my friend's husband, Peter, started pressuring me to book my train or bus ticket to Brussels. Despite my assurance that I could book it later and that we could proceed with other train tickets and hotel reservations for our onward journeys, Peter insisted that I booked it first and refused to proceed further with other hotel/train reservations on the onward journey. This was the second occasion; I noticed his tendency for me to book first before they made their own booking.

Peter began recommending late-night bus alternatives that could have brought me to Brussels ahead of their arrival, with some options being just two hours after their expected arrival. Despite my proposal to meet them at the hotel, the persistent senior citizen continued to pressure me into making a booking. Feeling pressured and stressed, I ultimately chose the option he recommended and made a reservation for a non-refundable night bus departing from Paris airport at midnight, with an arrival in Brussels at 3 AM.

Tip: You can reduce your hotel expenses by booking overnight train or bus journeys instead of daytime trips.

Two days after making the reservation, my neighbour Patricia shared recommendations ranging from dining options to sightseeing activities such as visiting Jungfrau and having breakfast at 007 Schilthorn. She also suggested a tip for visiting the Colosseum: to start following a tour group to learn about its history from the travel guide without incurring any additional costs.

Tip: Before your trip, gather advice on packing essentials, dining options, local customs, weather, and other travel tips by conducting an online search for insights on what to know before visiting your destination country.

Patricia recounted her recent experience at the Paris airport bus stop, where someone tried to snatch her bag during an evening bus journey. Fortunately, the intervention of other passengers saved her luggage. She strongly discouraged taking the bus at night, and suggested opting for a morning train instead. I subsequently briefed two of my former bosses about the situation, and both recommended booking a room at the Ibis Style hotel at the airport. I made my safety a top priority. Following my neighbour's advice, I booked a hotel and later rebooked a daytime train transfer, incurring extra costs and losing money on non-refundable tickets. All expenses totalling approximately 14k. While I don't regret the additional expenses, I do feel that they shouldn't have stressed that they would not proceed with future hotel bookings until I book my transfer to Brussels.

Tip: Searching for terms like "tourism traps" on Google for your destination can boost your awareness and help you take precautionary measures before your travel date, ensuring you have a thoroughly enjoyable vacation.

This incident made me realize that some individuals prioritize their own interests, convenience, and safety without considering the unique situation and safety concerns of a solo female traveller moving from one city to another. I couldn't help but ponder what might have gone wrong if he had allowed me the time to think and book my own train ticket later, especially considering my air tickets were already confirmed. Moreover, if he had given me the chance to carefully consider and book the ticket at my own pace, I wouldn't have harboured negative feelings toward him.

Tip: Refrain from pressuring others, especially in financial matters. Pressuring can lead to financial losses and strained relationships among individuals.

After completing train bookings, Peter insisted on hotel reservations. Booking the trip was tiresome for me as I struggled to understand whether they preferred cheaper accommodation or a 5-star hotel. For three consecutive days, I spent nearly 5.5 hours each day doing travel bookings, which is not my usual way of planning trips. My mom even noticed and mentioned that I had really stressful days.

When picking a hotel, I always consider its proximity to sightseeing spots and the accessibility of transportation. When booking a hotel in Rome, Annie found one we both liked at a good price. However, after reading the reviews, I pointed out to Annie that the hotel is situated quite far from the city centre in an industrial area, whereas most attractions are typically centralised. But she said the hotel was affordable, so we decided to book it anyway.

Annie and I had difficulty deciding which attractions to visit due to our limited time in Lucerne. So, I called the hotel before making reservations to ask about how to get there from the main station, the distance to sightseeing spots, and the transportation options available. After being convinced, we went ahead and booked the hotel for our stay in Lucerne.

Tip: If you're traveling to a new country and unsure about what activities to explore, consider reaching out to a confirmed hotel reservation. Inform them of your upcoming stay and feel free to inquire about sightseeing information or any other questions you may have.

During hotel reservations, I observed that whenever there were significant transactions in international currency, Peter urged me to use my credit card. Using a credit card for foreign transactions incurs a conversion fee. While Annie, Peter, and I were coordinating over the phone to make multiple reservations together, when it came to the last booking, we realized that anyone booking the resort would pay a heavy amount on credit card as we planned to stay maximum nights in that resort. It was Peter's turn to book the resort as I had made maximum reservations through my card. I asked Annie if Peter is booking the resort, however, Annie informed that Peter had already gone to sleep by then.

If Annie wished, she could have suggested delaying the booking until the morning, considering Peter had to make the reservation. Not wanting to spend more time searching for hotels and making lengthy calls, I promptly booked the resort using my credit card. Within seconds of my booking, Peter exclaimed, "Booking kar liya (is the booking done), let me check." After a few minutes, he claimed that Annie and I had booked at higher prices, while he found the same resort at a lower price on a different website. I offered to check if it was the same deal, and I could cancel my booking. However, he quickly added that the price was the same as the one I had booked Asking not to cancel. I had a strong gut feeling that Peter was pretending to be asleep or had Annie lie on the phone to avoid payment for this reservation, given its maximum price.

In the morning, Peter, in his excitement, mentioned buying 1000 euros at a cheaper rate. When I asked about the exchange rate, he claimed not to remember it. When friends travel together, they usually share the cost at which they bought currency, allowing others to buy at the same price. Hiding from co-traveller seemed strange.

Both instances—his refusal to disclose the currency rate and pretending to be asleep to evade making reservations—raised suspicions about Peter's motives. I had a strong sense something fishy was going on Peter's mind.

Tip: When traveling with a group of three consisting of one solo traveller and two individuals from the same family, it is best for all three to equally participate in securing reservations using their respective payment methods. This ensures fair distribution of financial responsibilities and prevents excessive blocking of funds on the solo traveller's card.

The next day, Annie mentioned that she had settled on an Airbnb for our Florence trip. Upon reviewing online feedback, I noted a recurring mention of men lingering outside the apartment, engaging in drinking and smoking, which raised concerns about safety. However, Annie, relying on her husband's judgment, felt comfortable with the choice, so I refrained from expressing further reservations after reading the reviews. Plus, since I hadn't booked any Airbnb accommodations before, I trusted them to handle the booking process.

Tip: Opting for Airbnb accommodations is often one of the most budget-friendly ways to travel. It's essential to thoroughly review and consider the ratings and prices.

Tip: When browsing hotels online, consider checking the three or four-star ratings and reading reviews. They provide valuable insights into the surroundings, distance to the city centre, transportation options, and share pros and cons about the property.

Observing the considerable daily time spent on travel arrangements with Annie and Peter, totalling 5.5 hours over the past few days and once consuming a full 8 hours equivalent to my work time, my mom considered opposing my participation in the trip. Concerned about Peter's persistent nature, she worried the trip might not be enjoyable if his behaviour continued. She knew that as a solo traveller, I usually don't spend that much time on bookings. Nonetheless, she chose not to explicitly voice her concerns to me.

Later that day, Peter and Annie called and suggested booking the Swiss pass. Getting the Swiss pass costs 25k, but if you combine it with sightseeing options, you'll get discounts on attractions. However, adding attractions could double the total cost of the Swiss pass to over 50k per person. Despite Peter's insistence, I didn't feel comfortable booking the Swiss pass without researching its benefits thoroughly. I suggested they proceed with their purchase, and I would consider it later.

Once all the arrangements were in place, I informed Annie about my weak knee, leading me to choose a lighter suitcase over a larger one to avoid lifting heavy weights. In return, she mentioned having a problem with her arm like a dislocated tissue, making it challenging for her to manage heavy loads.

Tip: Don't pressure others too hard. Sometimes people don't express their thoughts directly to be polite. If someone says they'll book reservations, give them the space to do it themselves.

Two days before the flight, I requested Annie to settle the bill to ensure no pendency of credit card payments in my absence. To my surprise, Peter replied that he had 1000 euros and planned to settle in euros while in Europe. Finding his behaviour strange, I called Annie and questioned her since we had agreed to settle transactions in INR to INR and euros to euros. I was puzzled as to why Peter was attempting to pay in euros for expenses in INR, especially after reaching our destination. Annie assured me and finally the transactions settled before our flights.

This incident led me to believe that Peter was quite clever:

1. He had me book the reservations with heavy payments, ensuring no immediate payment on his credit card.
2. As a businessman, he might possess undisclosed funds, referred to as black money, which he intends to use by paying for rupee transactions in Euros. This could be an attempt to avoid taxes by not declaring the black money in official records.
3. By purchasing euros at a lower rate without disclosing it, using them for my expenses allowed him to charge me at the current rate, indirectly extracting more money from me.

My best friend Sophie suggested cancelling the trip to Europe seeing me spending 6 hours daily to travel bookings, and I hadn't experienced stress over the years while planning travel arrangements. Sometimes a third person can view the situation more clearly than the person undergoing. In my case my mum and my friend Sophie both were not in favour of this trip looking at daily interaction with Peter. However, it seemed improbable for me to back out at this stage.

The friends you travel with can matter more than the country you're visiting

Settle bills before you head for your vacation:

1. Always notify your bank of your upcoming travel plans to other countries. This will prevent the bank from blocking your card due to unusual transactions abroad.
2. Settle your bills before departing. While it might not be your top priority, credit card companies may still levy interest and late fees if payments are missed while you're on vacation.

Starting from checking the expiration date of your passport to making all necessary bookings, here are some tips to help you plan your trip effectively:

1. Verify the expiration date of your passport. Immigration authorities may refuse entry if passports are due to expire within six months.
2. It's always a good idea to compare prices across different days and airlines to find the best deal for your specific travel plans.
3. Typically, when purchasing airline tickets online, the most significant price hikes occur around 2 weeks before your departure date.
4. When arranging a flight with a layover in the USA, remember that you'll generally need at least an hour and a half for the layover. Anything less might not provide sufficient time to catch the connecting flight.
5. When working with a travel agent, inquire about discounts on excursions, entertainment, and additional perks. Agents frequently have access to exclusive discounts and connections not available through online booking sites.
6. Always experiment with different departure dates when booking tickets online. Departing a day earlier or staying an extra day could help you save a lot of money on your ticket..

Ground rules

Some Ground Rules for Trips that I follow when I travel with others.

1. I meet co passengers directly at the boarding gate before the flight. Reason: immigration and security take time and I like to explore all the duty-free shops and spend good time at lounge. Usually, I prefer to reach 3 hours before flight which may not be the preference of others
2. We may have different seats on aircraft Reason: I prefer an aisle seat as I don't like to ask passengers to get up to go to restroom. I may also get an upgraded seat with or without fee and not necessarily others would be accommodated or their preferred choice
3. Pre-paid Taxi fare from airport to residence will be split equal at the airport itself
4. We fund our own lunches and dinner. I'm vegetarian on some days
5. If one happens to use a credit card instead of Forex or cash for someone else's need then there will be conversion charges too
6. We will make our own arrangements to meet our friends to some central location over inviting them to home/hotel
7. We will meet our friends/relatives solo to have our own space and privacy
8. During shopping, taste may vary so we will have the freedom to do our own shopping/stuff and decide on meeting at a central point at an agreed time

Feel free to make your own preferred choices.

Chapter 2

Through the Airport: From Check-in to Touchdown

I maintain a packing list and adjust it based on my experiences from each journey, it saves time and helps being organized for all travels.

- **Electronics** - iPhone pin changer, iPhone charger, mobile, tablet or laptop, Ear plugs, Apple Watch, Camera, Power backup, iPhone pin to switch SIMS
- **Identity** - License, Tickets and Passport, passport size photos, Vaccination certificate
- **Money**: Currency, Forex & Credit card
- **Packing**: Goggles, Cream, Comb, Earrings, Accessories and lipsticks, Shower cap, Pedicure brush, clothes and shoes, hand towel, Gloves, Belt, Safety pin, Nail cutter, Sanitary pads, Iron, Umbrella, Hat
- **Others:**
  - Prayer book
  - Download WhatsApp and Viber

- Buy Matrix for International Calls and Data
- Check the list of people for gifts
- Carry cooking recipes

I transfer pictures from my handset to laptop before traveling, as a backup.

I always pack enough clothes for the duration of my trip, plus a few extra T-shirts. After packing, I check the weight of my luggage to ensure it meets the airline's allowance, avoiding any extra fees or check-in issues.

Nowadays, web check-in simplifies the process by allowing timely check-in and seat selection, reducing one less thing to worry about. I had already checked in and having the printed boarding pass helps when going through the baggage counter, making it easy. Additionally, I saved a screenshot of the boarding pass on my mobile for convenience.

Tip: Various Airlines have apps that allow you to check in and print your boarding pass up to 24 hours before your departure time. This enables you to bypass the check-in line at the airport and head directly to the baggage drop area.

Tip: Don't forget to capture a screenshot of your mobile boarding pass before you leave for the airport. Relying on an internet connection to access it at the gate could cause unnecessary stress.

I had a morning flight decided to leave home at 7 AM, I didn't want to disturb my mum with cooking in the morning so told her that I will have my breakfast at the lounge as my HDFC Regalia credit card grants access to the airport's premium lounge at a nominal fee.

Before leaving from home, I checked travel documents thoroughly: Passport, visas, boarding passes, and any other required documents are in order. I secured valuables by keeping important items such as passports, wallets, and electronics in my hand carry. I usually aim to get to the airport early to have enough time for security checks, enjoy my time while having breakfast in lounge and any unexpected waits. I called my credit card companies to let them know about my travel plans to prevent any problems with my credit cards while I was abroad.

I attached a distinctive band to my luggage before going to baggage drop area so that I could easily identify it upon arrival in the destination country. I received the baggage tags and stored it safely in my purse.

Tip: Attach a brightly coloured ribbon to your bag to easily identify it at the baggage claim.

Tip: Snap a photo of your luggage claim ticket using your phone. It'll be useful if you misplace it and need to retrieve your luggage.

After I had successfully checked in my luggage, I inquired with the airline representative about the possibility of an upgrade. However, since the flight wasn't fully booked, the chances of an upgrade were slim.

Tip: Don't hesitate to inquire about an upgrade on your flight. Frequently, business or first class isn't fully booked, and some airlines may offer complimentary upgrades. The worst-case scenario is they decline, but at least you made the attempt.

After years of travelling, I found myself at the airport's currency exchange desk for only the second time, purchasing currency at the last minute. The representative initially offered 100 INR for 1 euro, but after some negotiation, we agreed on a final exchange rate of 97 INR.

Tip: Don't purchase currency at airports. The exchange rates they are typically the worst.

After securely stashing my currency in my purse and jeans, I proceeded towards immigration and security check. The economy line was as crowded as usual, so I made the decision to join the business line in order to speed up the process.

Tip: Joining the queue with business travellers can speed up your passage through security. They usually travel light, know the process well, and are often in a hurry, leading to faster clearance of the queue.

Tip: Keep your boarding pass readily available it helps save time.

By now, I've learned from experience that security may ask you to open your carry-on if they find items like a nail filer or liquids, perfumes, safety pins. Therefore, I always keep these items in a small pouch or zip lock bag and place it in one of the bins. This way, it's easier for the security staff to quickly inspect them without having me open my entire luggage.

Security

1. Put all loose items in your jacket pockets, and then place the jacket into a bin for security screening after immigration. This way, you won't have to empty it every time.

2. To accelerate airport security lines for yourself, figure out how many bins you'll need for screening: one for your backpack, another for electronics like laptop, cell phone, and watches, one for shoes, and one for your belt, wallet, and handbag.
3. Don't forget to bring an empty water bottle when you fly. Airports enforce strict regulations on liquids, even if it's just water. You can fill it up after clearing security.
4. Be mindful of permitted items on the plane and keep liquids and electronics easily accessible.

I ensured to secure my passport in the inside pocket of Jeans and headed for boarding. I decided to skip breakfast at Premium Lounge due to boarding constraints. Upon reaching the boarding gate, I discovered that the boarding was delayed due to the late arrival of the crew. With only 10 minutes remaining, I returned to the lounge. Despite the presence of queue, I politely approached both, the passengers and the attendant, explaining that my boarding was about to commence and inquired if I could be accommodated first. They agreed and once inside the restaurant, I asked the hostess for a takeaway box. I packed pasta as I'm not particularly fond of Indian food, along with a water bottle and a can of Coke. Knowing that breakfast would be served on the flight after an hour and a half, I anticipated that my packed food would suffice.

Tip: A zipper pocket inside your jeans serves as an effective hiding spot for your passport and cash while traveling.

Tip: Always request people if they accommodate skipping queue or pack food (even if it's not their policy), you will be surprised when people accommodate your request.

Boarding was seamless for me, and being from the aviation industry, I found it convenient to secure an exit row seat with extra legroom at no additional cost. Throughout the flight, I enjoyed pleasant interactions with the crew. They even provided some small goodies for my nephew to take home, which was a nice gesture.

Tip: Certain airlines offer complimentary items for kids, such as small plane, games, cards. Simply ask a crew to provide them. You don't ask, you don't get.

I utilised my time in creating a list of people for whom I had to get a gift.

Tip: Before you leave, make a list of friends and family you want to buy souvenirs for. This will help you avoid forgetting someone's gift or regretting it later.

Being in the air gives me a completely different feeling, brimming with excitement as I eagerly anticipate exploring the other side of the world and interacting with the crew members. This connection still keeps me close to the aviation industry, despite having changed professions and no longer working in that field. After enjoying a delicious lunch, I typically place a special meal request before my departure, I decided to take a short nap. I felt relaxed knowing that I had already downloaded various applications such as currency converter, free video or text calling etc. to help make my travel journey smoother, alleviating one less thing to worry about.

Tip: Before embarking on your vacation, it's important to:

1. Download the XE Currency app for real-time currency rates.
2. Download apps that enable free video calls, texting, and instant messaging. Some recommended apps Viber, Signal, WhatsApp, or Skype on your phone are free.
3. Download the Google Translate app. Its camera feature allows you to point it at items such as menus, and street signs, providing real-time translations.

Upon landing, I made my way to immigration in Paris. Luckily, there wasn't a long queue, so I cleared it swiftly and proceeded to the arrival hall to collect my luggage. Spotting my bag was effortless due to the colorful band I had attached to it. As a precaution, I always double-check the baggage tag to confirm my name is on it after retrieving it. After all, nobody wants to go through the inconvenience of mistakenly taking someone else's luggage and then having to track down their own.

Tip: Before leaving the arrival hall, always double-check the name on the baggage tag to avoid the inconvenience of mistakenly taking someone else's bag and then having to search for your own bag to return theirs.

I glanced at my watch intending to adjust the time for Paris, but then realized that my phone automatically updates its time based on the current country's timezone.

Tip: The Apple phone's smart features automatically adjust to your current time zone (destination time zone), eliminating the need to manually adjust your watch.

More useful tips:

1. Avoid touching your face and eyes during travel, as it's an easy way for germs to enter your system. If you need to sneeze and lack a mask, utilize your elbow to cover your mouth.
2. Keep yourself hydrated.
3. Regularly washing your hands or carrying hand sanitizer is the most effective method to be clear of germs.

After clearing immigration, I had difficulty finding the IBIS hotel. There was one at the adjacent terminal, while the other was a 10-minute drive away, requiring me to take a shuttle outside the terminal. The shuttle service charges a nominal fee of 7-8 euros and conveniently drops you off at the hotel entrance. Upon arrival at the hotel, I also reserved my spot for the early morning shuttle, as my train was scheduled to depart from Paris airport to Brussels Midi. I rested for a few hours, I found that a good night's sleep always leaves you feeling fresher. I woke up early, got ready, had breakfast, and then returned to the same spot to wait for the shuttle. The shuttle dropped me off at the terminal, where I checked the display screen for information about the train platform. The journey was expected to take two hours.

Transportation Dilemmas: Taxi or Train, and Handling Cash

During this Europe trip, I planned to meet Annie and Peter at Brussels Central Station. Upon reaching Brussels Midi, I had to change trains within a tight window of 4 minutes to travel from Midi to Central Station. Unfortunately, it took longer than expected, and I ended up missing the train. I approached one of the train staff at the station to inquire about purchasing a new ticket for the next train. They reassured me that my tickets were valid for the entire day, and I could board any train. Additionally, they mentioned that the Central Station was just the next stop, with only a 3-minute train ride away.

I met Peter and Annie at the Brussels Central Station, they had large suitcases and a small duffel bag, while I had a medium sized stroller and hand luggage. At first, my friend Annie recommended getting an Uber, and I proceeded to book one. Regrettably, the driver arrived at the rear of the station and subsequently cancelled the ride. Confronted with this scenario, we had two choices: either book another Uber or walk to our destination. Peter, my friend's husband, favoured walking, so we opted to give it a shot. He suggested using Google Maps for directions on my mobile, and I followed them. Unaware that my default setting from my home country was for car navigation, I didn't realize Google Maps was providing directions meant for a car.

Tip: Before following directions on Google Maps, make sure to check if the directions are set for driving, walking, or public transportation like trains.

While Peter showed a bit of irritation, Annie stayed composed and proposed relying on walking directions instead of those intended for vehicles like cars, buses, or trains. I admired Annie's navigation skills and technical expertise, seizing the chance to learn something new from her. I started enthusiastically acknowledging Annie for her intelligence. Typically, when someone is praised in a group, it sparks others to join in and boost morale. However, in this instance, the dynamics were unique – Peter swiftly changed the topic. I felt Peter might be either jealous of his wife or reluctant to let her shine or take the lead in fear of losing dominance if she outsmarts him.

Following our hotel check-in, I wasn't hungry, having indulged in a buffet breakfast in Paris. Annie mentioned they hadn't eaten since the flight and planned to snack on the home-cooked bread she had brought before exploring the city. Annie gave packed rotis that could last for 20 days to be kept with me and utilise if feel hungry. I'm not a fan of Indian food and especially outside country I like to try new cuisine. I accepted it and just kept it in my luggage.

As we left the hotel for sightseeing, Peter once again requested the use of my Google Maps for navigation to the main pentagon and Grand Place. I began to sense his goal of saving on data costs, explaining why he consistently asked me to use my Google Maps for navigation. In contrast, my preference is to enjoy city exploration without heavy reliance on Google navigation, immersing myself in the streets, shops, and the overall experience.

Tip: Switch off Google Maps to have an authentic experience of the city. Taking leisurely walks around a city is one of the most effective methods to truly immerse yourself in the culture and engage with locals.

Tip: Before your trip, make sure to discuss international data and calling plans with all travellers. Agree on a usage strategy to prevent one traveller with limited data from running out and to ensure seamless communication throughout the journey.

FOOD

In the afternoon, they wanted a snack. While sharing is often seen as caring, things have changed after COVID. It's not safe to share food from one plate to another. I'm careful about not eating from someone else's plate or letting others eat from mine, especially because I'm single and don't have support system that married couples might have and health is important, especially after COVID.

Upon entering McDonald's, when asked about my food preference, I opted for a McFlurry as I had already enjoyed a substantial meal at the hotel in Paris. However, Peter suggested ordering one McFlurry and one serving of French fries. I couldn't fathom the idea of three people sharing only one McFlurry and a portion of French fries. Experiencing discomfort, I proposed that they use a separate ordering machine, and I would place my order independently. Upon receiving my order, I offered them a spoon, though I had no intention of sampling their food. Also, I thought that what they ordered might not be enough for a full meal for two people.

Within two hours, another incident related to food transpired. Peter recommended ordering a single portion of Belgium fries, 'La Friteries,' to share among the three of us. In my view, this wasn't appropriate as it wouldn't have been sufficient to satisfy anyone's hunger. Luckily, a lady at the counter alerted us that the fries contained beef oil, prompting us to decide against purchasing them.

At 5 pm, we decided to have dinner at a Chinese restaurant renowned for its delicious meal bowls. When the husband inquired about our meal choices, I explicitly mentioned that they could decide on their meals, and I needed some time to make my selection. They chose to share a meal bowl between the two of them, while I independently ordered my own Chinese meal bowl.

This was the first time they saw I could easily finish a whole meal by myself. On the other hand, I noticed they liked saving money by sharing dishes between the three of us. They would even split a meal into two parts if I didn't want to join, instead of ordering two separate meals.

Before our trip, we made some bookings together and some separately. I explicitly stated we'd settle Euro expenses in Euro and INR expenses in INR. I told Annie that we'd handle our own expenses for things like meals and shopping since I was alone, while she was with her husband. Before our flights, I shared an Excel sheet with our spending details to settle dues. Unfortunately, there was a mistake – it said I owed Annie 9 euros, but in reality, it was Annie who owed me 9 euros. It seemed Annie showed the Excel sheet to her husband, who is financially focused. But she forgot to tell him about the typing mistake, and actually, they owed me the euros.

We enjoyed a leisurely walk through the streets of Brussels, capturing great photos. Being a fan of Hard Rock Cafe, we decided to go. Annie didn't order anything, I ordered coffee, and Peter had a beer. What struck me as odd was Peter's comment that I owed them 9 euros, despite my prior clarification that they owed me. I chose to disregard his comment without responding. Annie had the opportunity to correct Peter but chose to remain silent.

While at the Chocolate Museum in Brussels, Peter commented that there was a long queue, suggesting to skip it without asking for our opinions. I agreed, mostly because my friend Annie followed her husband's lead. At this point, it was becoming clear that Peter liked taking charge, making decisions without consulting, and seemed dominant in our group.

Tip: To avoid confusion and ensure clarity with fellow travellers, it's crucial to openly communicate your preferences and desires.

As we strolled back to the hotel, they purchased a pet bottle of Coke from a shop. Approaching a corner, I suggested turning left, but Peter insisted on going in the opposite direction. It was the first time I noticed he liked doing the opposite of what's suggested.

In the evening, they came to my room with their Coke, took a few sips, and placed the bottle on the side table. I didn't drink it because I prefer coffee. Peter talked about taking the tram or bus to the station for next day's train journey to Amsterdam but Annie said we should take a taxi, and I agreed.

At 9 pm, they went to their room and forgot to carry their Coke bottle. About 30 minutes later, Peter came to get it and I handed it over. I found it somewhat lacking in courtesy that Annie didn't come herself and instead sent her husband Peter to a lady's room late at night. I wondered why it couldn't wait until morning, maybe thinking I might drink the Coke while asleep. Next morning, I reached the restaurant for breakfast, Annie and Peter were yet to join. I enjoyed different variety of fruits and cereals.

Tip: Incorporate fruits into your daily diet. Enjoy them either during the complimentary breakfast offered by your hotel or purchase them from a grocery store if staying at an Airbnb.

After breakfast, we decided a short walk around the hotel to click some pics and enjoyed the great weather with few people around. We saw colourful buildings depicting ships and the sea during our stroll. Suddenly, Peter noticed a tram station and suggested using it for our journey to the station. He even figured out that it would cost less than 12 euros for all three of us. Although I was okay with their decision, my friend Annie insisted on sticking with the taxi plan. When we got back to the hotel, both Peter and I asked the receptionist about the taxi fare. The receptionist said it would be between 10-14 euros, and he started calling for a taxi. However, Peter quickly interrupted, saying we would let him know shortly as we still had to check out our luggage. Peter's actions were confusing, making me think he might be finding the cost too much; otherwise, he would have said to book a taxi in 15 minutes. I went downstairs with my bags and finished checking out. While waiting for Annie and Peter, I ordered a coffee. The waitress was friendly, and we chatted about catching a train from Brussels Midi. I also asked her the easiest way to get there, and she said the underground train is fast and direct. She further shared it would cost 7 euros for all three of us. In the meantime, Peter joined us. I briefed him of the conversation and suggested to speak to the hostess for more details, I went to get a map of Brussels because I like collecting them. I returned, but Peter still didn't clearly say we'd take a cab.

I wanted to talk to Annie, but she was busy chatting with other guests of Indian origin. I went back to the hostess and said I haven't spoken to Annie yet. The hostess offered to take us to the underground train entrance and said she'd be back after letting her colleague know she'd be away for a bit. She arranged for someone else to cover her. I asked Peter if he informed Annie about the plan, but he stayed silent. Annie was deeply engaged in a conversation. Feeling it would be impolite to interrupt, I patiently waited, hoping she would notice me.

In the meanwhile, without my request, the hostess took my bags and asked me to follow her. She moved swiftly, and I had to hurry to keep up. It left me torn between chasing my bags or go back to hotel to inform Annie of the change in plans. I kept looking back to see if Annie and Peter had come out of the hotel. Suddenly, I saw them coming. There was a 100 feet gap, so they started following me to catch up. I signalled that we should follow the hostess.

Strangely, neither of them, tried to phone me or proposed taking a taxi. When we got close to the underground station, I asked the hostess for her name and told her I'd give positive feedback. It was a way for me to chat briefly while waiting for Annie and Peter. The hostess and I used the escalator which was easy with only one bag. We waited for them near the bottom of the escalator.

Peter assisted Annie on the escalator and put her big suitcase on the same stepper of escalator she was standing on. Since escalators keep moving, Annie was not able to hold the bag properly on escalator and started losing balance. The hostess was helpful to offer that she will go up and get their bags, but seeing my friend losing balance I started running backwards to help her on the escalator.

In so much of two blocks and hustle bustle, it made me understand her age might be affecting her ability to travel comfortably. Anyhow we came down finally.

The hostess led us to the ticket counter, and Peter began extracting a few euros from his pocket, including several 10- or 20-euro bills. I always keep a ten euro in my right pocket for quick purchases, so I told Peter we'd sort it out later, and I'd pay for the tickets. Showing money in public can be risky as it may invite trouble; even Annie chimed in, advising him to put it back.

Tip: When traveling abroad, prioritize using credit cards over debit cards and cash. While lost money or misuse of a debit card can't be recovered, if a credit card is stolen, you have the option to dispute any unauthorized purchases.

We got on the train. I observed that Annie looked stressed and, through her facial expression indicated that she was wearing valuable diamond jewellery. Prior to the trip, I advised Annie not to carry expensive jewellery due to the situation in Europe. Had I known that she was carrying expensive jewels, I would have insisted on taxi and ignored the confusing actions of Peter. I felt bad that an older lady had to deal with the hurry and risk on the escalator.

When we arrived at Brussels main station, we had to carry our luggage up the stairs to get to the platform for the train to Antwerp Central. I assisted Peter with his bags. We waited for the incoming train to arrive.

Despite sensing that Annie was hassled, scared, and possibly annoyed with the rush, she didn't show or blamed me. Instead, I took full responsibility and apologised to Annie, acknowledging that I should have been more considerate of her age and travel limitations when rushing. I noticed Peter didn't say anything about Annie falling on the escalator. I wondered if it was because he felt guilty or if he stayed quiet to save a few pennies.

Knowing the couple is senior, I decided to let them make decisions without my input. This was to prevent problems, accusations, and stay 'neutral' on everything they asked.

I kept my frustrations regarding Peter's conflicting/ confusing actions to myself. For instance, he stopped the receptionist from calling a taxi, yet during our morning walk, he discussed using trams and metros, showing he wasn't sure about taking a taxi and was considering other options to reach Midi station. Normally, when we're certain about taking a taxi, we wouldn't discuss alternative options, inquire about other transportation methods, or calculate costs. In this case, his indecision and mixed signals caused confusion and morning chaos for everyone.

It will become evident in upcoming chapters that he rarely listened to his wife and often did the opposite of what she suggested.

Furthermore, when descending on an escalator, the responsibility for managing baggage and ensuring safety rests with the person assisting, not the person standing at the bottom of the escalator. In this case, the husband didn't make sure his wife and the baggage were safely positioned on the escalator, leading to his wife losing balance.

It's possible that they believed I was waiting at the bottom of the escalator, hence they rushed. However, it's worth noting that the city's trains have a high frequency, and we wouldn't have missed any train if they had taken a few more minutes to ensure safety and comfort.

Towards the end of the trip and the last chapters of this book, it did strike me that throughout our entire European journey, we relied on trains for transportation between various destinations, often for longer durations with luggage. So, it was somewhat surprising to witness their discomfort in taking a train for just one segment and then sharing the incident with their friends at their next destination, making me appear as the one at fault. It certainly gave me something to ponder.

Tip: Always keep loose currency in front pockets.

Invest in yourself through travel experiences.

Chapter 3

Travel tips and tricks: Luggage handling, VAT eligibility, room security, train discounts and safety measures.

The following day, we embarked on a train journey to another city in Belgium. Annie and I had different objectives for our trip. They were attending a family reunion, while my goal was to explore and enjoy the city.

While we were on the train together, they received a text from the event coordinator informing them that there wouldn't be a taxi at the train station, which left them feeling disappointed. I said they should call their cousin to double-check the plans since he promised to arrange a pickup before their Europe trip began. Talking on the phone is usually clearer than texting. Despite that, Peter opted to text his cousin, and the response was a promise to refund the money of taxi.

Upon disembarking, Peter joked about leaving his phone behind, trying to get sympathy. Annie and I were surprised, but we found out later that he was just kidding. We thought such jokes were unnecessary because sometimes what you say in jest can unexpectedly become reality. Surprisingly, he got mugged in less than 5 days.

Upon arrival at Antwerp Central, we parted ways as they had a family reunion to attend while I had my own plans. We arranged our own taxis, and mine arrived first. Although Annie's was still en route, I bid them farewell. The taxi driver, of African descent, promptly stowed my luggage in the trunk, which made me uneasy as I prefer to keep it within sight. I noticed him making adjustments on his Uber app, which raised my suspicions. While checking the route on Uber, I realized he veered left instead of right. When I questioned him, he cited traffic as the reason for the deviation. Upon reaching the hotel. The driver parked car on the pavement of the hotel. He demanded cash payment of 17 euros, contrary to the 14 euros indicated on the Uber app while booking. I insisted that app showed 14 euros and payment was through credit card, leading to a debate where he claimed 17 euros were due, pointing to his mobile screen with 17 euros cash payment. Aware of the travel risks, I strategically always keep spare change in my pocket to avoid revealing the location of my wallet. I informed him of having 20 euros, demanding change before payment. To my surprise he informed not having the change of 20 euros. He popped open the trunk without stepping out of the car, which made me concerned that if I handed over the cash and got out, he might speed off, leaving me without my luggage. This hotel lacked security measures such as guards or separate entry and exit points common in hotels in India or the USA. Concerned about potential foul play, I opted to retrieve change from the reception rather than completing the transaction outside. I also asked him to retrieve my bag from the trunk. He quickly searched for change in the dashboard of his car, exited the car, and extracted my luggage from trunk. I paid him 20 euros, and he promptly returned the change which was less by few pennies but I didn't bother.

Tip:

1. Request the driver to keep the luggage inside the car rather than placing it in the boot.
2. Ask the driver to remove the luggage from the boot before making the payment.

After check-in, I went to my room and inspected its safety. I noticed that European hotel rooms are generally smaller compared to those in the USA or India. I observed a glass window without a latch, making it vulnerable to break-ins. Moreover, despite my room being on the second floor, the adjacent building had a large terrace on the first floor, with movable steel staircases lying in corner. This meant there was only one floor's difference between that terrace and my room, making it easier for someone to attempt a break-in.

Peter called to share that they reached their hotel safely and invited me over. Even though I had no initial intentions of visiting Annie at their hotel, as I preferred my own freedom and space, they insisted that I come over. When we were in Brussels, Peter was dependent on my data plan for road navigation, which led to exceeding my data allowance, especially with the additional navigation to their hotel in Antwerp. Therefore, to conserve data, I adopted a strategy of referring to Google maps to obtain the route, taking a picture of it, and then closing the app. I then navigated the streets by enlarging the captured picture and following the correct directions.

Tip: Take a picture of the direction list and look at it as a photo. Viewing a photo consumes significantly less battery than running google maps.

When I reached their hotel, they proudly displayed the luxury of their accommodations and the variety of complimentary snacks available in their room. I was pleased and happy that they both would have a relaxed time with their family now. They asked me to carry the snacks to lighten their load for the next day and to store stuff for onward journey. I made sure to give them snacks whenever they wanted during our journey.

Peter expressed regret for not calling his cousin. Upon arriving at the hotel, the cousin revealed they had arranged a car to pick up passengers from Brussels airport to Antwerp in the morning, indicating that they could have travelled comfortably from Brussels Midi to Antwerp instead of traveling via Train. I wondered why Peter didn't call his cousin when I suggested it. If he had called, he would've known about transportation. By this time, my impression of my friend's husband Peter was solidifying – it seemed he didn't like taking advice, often did the opposite, and only regretted it later.

I left from the hotel and leisurely explored all the nearby attractions. Earlier in the morning I had taken a map from the hotel, and a representative had marked all the nearby attractions that were within walking distance, facilitating easy navigation. The Antwerp Center emerged as the focal point, boasting an array of branded shops perfect for shopping enthusiasts. I visited Armani Exchange and purchased two purses, one for myself and one for my friend. Mine was a backpack-style purse, while my friend's was more of a tote bag. The shopkeeper kindly reminded me about the VAT and suggested getting it refunded, even though VAT refunds aren't applicable for shopping in the USA. However, he refreshed my memory about VAT refunds from a previous European trip. He explained that to claim the VAT refund, the minimum purchase value had to exceed 150-200 euros. He then took my passport details, filled out the necessary form, and handed me the envelope to claim the refund at the airport on the day of my departure flight. After shopping, I returned to my hotel and rested.

Tip: Always check with stores regarding VAT eligibility. It's crucial to provide your passport number when filling out the form for VAT refunds.

While planning the European trip, Annie and Peter had declined to visit Bruges because they preferred to spend more time in Amsterdam. They worried that adding Bruges to the itinerary might need an overnight stay, but my research said it's doable in a day from Antwerp or Brussels. The next day, I decided to do a day trip from Antwerp to Bruges. I was worried about leaving my luggage and expensive Armani gifts unattended in the room, especially since the glass window lacked a latch and the stairs outside suggested easy access to my room if someone attempted to enter through the window. To address this, I quickly took action by placing my suitcase under the bed and arranging a layer of sheets to make it appear as though the room was unused. Additionally, I noticed that the TV cabinet had open side shelves, and the hotel had placed an extra pillow on one of them. I decided to conceal the Armani bags behind the pillow shelf, so anyone attempting to peek inside would get the impression that the room was unoccupied.

Being weekend, I got 50% discount on the train ticket. Also, there was a deal for couples: buy one ticket, get one free on weekends. If Annie and Peter had followed my suggestion to include a day in Bruges and cut a day from Amsterdam, they would have benefited. Regardless, it's their missed opportunity.

During the train journey from Antwerp Central to Bruges, a person sat across from me and we exchanged smiles. My usual preference in clothing is to adopt a hippie style, with my hair tied up on top and fanned out across my head. However, after some time, he began to use marijuana. I politely excused myself and moved to another seat on the train. I noticed that he disembarked at the next stop.

Upon reaching the Brugge station, I walked confidently to avoid appearing like a tourist, but inadvertently exited from what seemed to be the rear side. Upon re-entering, I visited a shop offering various vacation packages for trains and buses. Inquiring about local attractions, I acquired a map, which surprisingly didn't cost a penny, unlike in cities like Prague where maps can cost up to 1 euro. Exiting from the front of the station this time, I was pleased to see lots of tourists heading in the same direction, so I confidently continued my journey along with them.

Tip: Walk like you know where you're going: Look confident and determined when you walk, even if you're unsure. Try not to use maps or guidebooks while walking around.

Bruges is a must-visit, and I really enjoyed sightseeing there. I happily visited 10 museums and gladly paid for each. In contrast, they mainly discussed the possibility of doing activities such as bicycle ride in Amsterdam but were less inclined to spend money on activities. I came across a traveling group, near the canal ride. I bought my ticket and stood in line with the group and their travel guide. I noticed tour guide taking awesome pictures of his group while we were waiting to get on the canal. I asked for a photo, and it turned out really nice. However, be careful before handing over your camera to strangers. The muggers travelling in groups can swiftly pass your phone among themselves without realising it. During the conversation the tour guide recommended that, as a solo traveller, I must carry a stick to avoid being a victim of theft and asked to join their group to enjoy some attractions together.

Tip: Carry a folding stick, if traveling solo

During the canal ride, the boat can accommodate 20-30 passengers in an open boat. Typically, sitting at the end or in the front after the boat driver offers the best view, but I chose to sit in the middle because I enjoy taking pictures and videos of the surroundings. It felt risky to sit on the left or right seats because if my phone fell into the water while taking pictures due to any sudden movements, it could have been a problem. After all, my phone is the only way to stay connected with my family and loved ones, and it contains all the important documents, so it would have been troublesome if something happened to it.

After the canal ride, the tour guide kindly offered to let me stick with their group since I was solo and see the attractions along with them. I continued with them for 5 minutes, but then I spotted a church and decided to enter and admire the architectural work.

By afternoon, the streets were bustling with crowds. On the way, I passed by an open market, but nothing caught my eye enough to make a purchase. I also visited a museum where they displayed the tools used to punish the offenders during medieval times. The sight was certainly disturbing, and I wouldn't recommend it for people with a weak heart to visit.

I also stumbled upon a shop that had unique items like small umbrellas, shoes, Christmas trees, and more, all made of stiff fabric, perfect for displaying on your desk.

There was a hospital that was converted into a museum, where you could buy an entry ticket to learn about how sugar affects different parts of your body. I decided to skip it since that's not my area of interest.

I really wanted to go for a horse-drawn carriage ride, so I went to De Markt, where you'll find Belfort and a place with lots of restaurants and carriage rides. I noticed there was a long line, so I opted to visit Belfort first. Belfort is like the Qutub Minar in Delhi. When I got to the ticket counter, the attendant informed me that I'd need to return in an hour because the maximum number of visitors allowed at the top of the Belfort was already reached. I had limited time in Bruges since I planned to catch the return train to Antwerp by 4:20 PM or at the latest by 5:20 PM. I always keep two timings in mind; if I miss one, then I make sure not to miss the next one. Deciding to come back in an hour didn't seem practical to me. I always like to give things a try. If it works out, great, but even if it doesn't, I find satisfaction in knowing that I tried. I asked the representative at the ticket counter if they could accommodate one more passenger, emphasizing that it wouldn't make much difference since I was traveling solo. He agreed and asked me to wait for 15 minutes so that 1-2 passengers could come down before allowing me to go up. I was fortunate to avoid an hour of waiting and purchased the ticket to ascend to the top of Belfort. The stairs are round and steep, with a rope next to them for support. I wouldn't recommend elderly people visit the top to admire the view as it can be risky. There's a huge bell at the top of the tower, and you get an amazing view of the entire city from up there. After I came down, I checked again to see if I could get a horse carriage ride, but it just wasn't my day as all the carriages were full.

Tip: Always politely ask if there's a chance of being accommodated; you might get lucky and avoid waiting for an hour. This approach can be particularly helpful if you're traveling solo.

I decided to visit the Basilica of the Holy Blood, which is known for housing a cloth stained with what is believed to be the actual blood of Christ. The cloth is kept inside a glass container for people to view in line before moving on. Taking photos is not allowed. You can visit this place and explore it within 10 minutes.

On my way back to the train station, I stumbled upon Lover's Point. The canals, bridges, and Lover's Point all reminded me of a movie titled "PK". Lover's Point was a small bridge and a spot perfect for taking pictures. While I was at Lover's Bridge, I saw a group of three girls, with one of them taking nice pictures of her friend. I decided to recreate the same pose for a picture and asked the girl taking the photo if she could take one of me too, so I handed her my camera. One of the girls, who was a bit heavier, also asked for my jacket and small bag containing snacks, water, and souvenirs. Although it made me a little nervous to hand over my belongings, the steady stream of people on the small bridge lowered the chance of anything bad happening.

Tip: Evaluate your surroundings before handing over your belongings.

En route, I saw Begijnhof, one of the heritage sites used by nuns. It's a spacious area enveloped by greenery. There are about 30 houses painted in white surrounding a central courtyard. The entrance gate proudly displayed a significant number 1776, marking the year of its construction. Visitors can enter through this gate and exit from the other one.

I was in a hurry to catch my train, so I needed to find someone quickly without taking any risks. I approached an Indian woman and asked her to take a photo for me on the canal bridge to capture a clear view of the entrance gate with the 1776 number. I relied on the "brotherhood in a foreign land" notion, trusting that she would take good pictures and wouldn't run away with my phone.

My battery was low from taking so many pictures, but I still used it for navigation, when necessary, quickly checking the road and then putting the phone away. Along the way to the train station, I stopped at restaurants where the waiter was on a break to smoke, just to make sure I was heading in the right direction. I asked him for directions to the train station, and he kindly guided me.

Tip: Seek directions politely: If you're lost, ask locals for help in a friendly and subtle manner, as if you're just double-checking even though you know the area.

In between I quickly opened Google Maps to find my way to the train station and managed to arrive on time. Having the return ticket was helpful because you can go directly to the platform instead of standing in the queue at the train station, avoiding last-minute hassle.

While in Bruges, waiting for the train to Antwerp, I stood near the staircase. I usually use earplugs to talk, keeping my phone in my pocket or purse. As I stood next to the uncovered staircase, I tend to pace around while talking. At one point, I turned and found myself facing the staircase. My earplug was slightly loose, and suddenly, it struck me that the train was approaching. I had a moment of concern about what I would do if my earplug fell onto the stairs - leave it or miss the train? It was at that moment I realized one should avoid standing near staircases, a thought I had even before the mugging incident, and I shared this observation with Annie and Peter as well.

Upon returning to the hotel from Bruges at approximately 7:30 PM, I was relieved to see my stuff intact. I decided to go lobby to fetch some water. As the elevator doors opened, I encountered two individuals of African descent who were leaving the elevator. Out of my usual habit, we exchanged greetings, but it prompted me to consider being more cautious when traveling alone and staying in accommodations that might have limited security measures.

Upon refilling my water bottle and returning to my floor, I encountered both men from the elevator again, which surprised me. This time, I opted to ignore them, trusting my intuition that they might be going to the same floor with intentions of finding my room. To stay safe, I stood close to elevator and started a phone call. Eventually, they grasped that I wouldn't budge, prompting them to go downstairs.

I hurried back to my room, making sure to minimize any noise. Later, I found out those guys' room was either right across from mine or just one room away. Following day, I had plans to meet my friend at the train station to catch a 7 AM train to Amsterdam, so started packing my belongings in preparation for an early checkout. When Peter called to confirm our meeting time, he noticed I was speaking quietly. I explained that I was being cautious not to let others know I was alone in the room. However, his response involved some playful tone, as he implied there was no reason to be anxious and that nothing untoward would occur. At that moment, I wasn't in the mood for humour, and I felt relieved when he passed the phone to Annie. Thankfully, she understood my concern, confirmed our meeting time without making light of the situation. She even offered that I could call her if needed.

Though I understand his intent might have been to make me feel better, it's important for people to understand that a woman's safety worries are real. It's not a good idea to downplay these concerns during such moments. Jokes should consider the timing and context, as not everyone might feel comfortable with them, especially in certain situations.

Tip: When it comes to women's safety concerns, it's crucial not to minimize or downplay these worries. Avoid making jokes in such situations.

The next day, at 6 AM, I took my luggage downstairs and left it at the front desk for an early check-out. After having breakfast, I grabbed two chocolate croissants for my train ride to Amsterdam. It takes about 15 minutes to walk to the train station. During this walk, there were very few people around, and a couple of individuals who looked sketchy, which could understandably make anyone feel a bit nervous.

Fortunately, I decided to walk alongside a tall middle-aged man. I matched my steps with his, and as we got closer to the train station, we exchanged looks. I thanked him for walking together and shared that sometimes it's wise to appear like you're with someone to avoid uncomfortable situations. He completely understood, and we chatted casually about work while walking before saying goodbye.

Since I had no more data, I used Starbucks Wi-Fi to tell Annie and Peter I reached the train station. Being polite,

I chose to buy a big sandwich for my lunch instead of just using the Wi-Fi without making a purchase. Peter came to Starbucks by himself, asked what I bought, and I pointed to the sandwich in the display and said I got it for my lunch. Afterward, he walked with me to where Annie was waiting with two suitcases.

Tip: Starbucks, McDonalds are the best places to access free Wi-Fi.

During our train journey from Antwerp to Amsterdam, I stressed the importance of not standing close to staircases. I explained that it's easy for potential thieves to throw something onto the staircase, and one of their accomplices can swiftly grab it and escape unnoticed. Victims usually focus on the people present on the platform, not realizing the thief used the staircase to exit.

Peter inquired about my previous day's activities. When I told him I went to Bruges, he seemed surprised. I explained that I had taken pictures of all the attractions and museums, so they could experience it visually, even if they couldn't visit in person. The Bell Tower is particularly famous, and I showed them pictures of the climb to the top, but I didn't recommend it due to the steep stairs, especially considering their age. I suggested they enjoy the view through the pictures instead.

I further added that I didn't find many activities to do in Antwerp, and I had always wanted to see Bruges since my friends had highly recommended it. I favour day trips over frequent city-to-city moves with luggage because it's time-saving and feels more efficient. I also reminded them that prior to the trip, Peter and Annie talked about wanting to visit Bruges on their next European trip.

Peter explained he liked staying in one place to avoid the one-hour commute in the mornings and evenings. Travelers always have varying perspectives, preferences, and travel styles that suit them best. I just said 'okay' to what he said and didn't say more because I liked having the freedom to go to Bruges on my own terms. I had the opportunity to explore the city, seeing at least 10 attractions. I bought tickets for churches, a canal ride, museums, and did some shopping. I took my time at each place as much as I wanted.

In the first two days of our trip, I quickly grasped that if I offered my opinion on anything, he could blame me for anything unfavourable. So, I made a deliberate choice to stay neutral and support whatever choices they made as the last thing one would want is to hear someone souring the mood by blaming others for things not going as per him. I figured this out from the start.

Traveling abroad, far from your home country, allows you to discover more about yourself as you journey

Chapter 4

Dealing with Theft and Deception: Concealing Travel Details, and Handling Accusations.

I typically don't revisit places I've previously visited. But, since they wanted to stay longer in Amsterdam due to acquaintances, even though I had been to Amsterdam on multiple occasions, I agreed to join them.

We arrived in Amsterdam and finalised our hotel check-in, hotel was located near the Schiphol airport. I also prioritize personal space and independence while traveling and had informed Annie beforehand that I would require some time to freshen up and settle, allowing them to go ahead and reunite with their acquaintances at the airport. Right before they left from the hotel, they notified me, and I reciprocated by letting them know that I'd meet up with them in approximately an hour at the airport. I assumed that due to their trip from India to Amsterdam, their acquaintances might treat them to lunch at Schiphol Airport, which is known for its diverse dining options.

When I met them at designated point at Schiphol Airport, Annie introduced me to her acquaintances and after exchanging greetings, they left. I suggested heading to the city centre, but Annie inquired if I still had a Starbucks sandwich since they were hungry. I explained that I had already eaten Starbucks sandwich but offered two croissants saved from breakfast indicating they could each have one.

It is genuinely astonishing that despite their wealth, they didn't choose to try the airport's restaurants. It's a fair expectation that everyone should cover their own meals when traveling to avoid any sense of obligation.

Tip: Avoid asking fellow travellers to buy you meals unless you've run out of money.

Moreover, it's essential for travellers to be financially prepared for their trips, including having enough money to purchase their own meals, to ensure their well-being. If you can't afford basic things like buying food or have to share one burger for lunch or dinner, it can cause health problems. It's really important for each traveller to manage their own expenses and well-being during a trip.

Throughout the trip, I had consistently maintained my practice of savoring my meals without sharing or offering, indicating that everyone should cover their own food costs. Despite this, they continued to try to save on their food expenses.

Purchasing tickets ahead of them

When we bought the day pass at a store in Schiphol airport, Peter, suggested a good idea: to get a one-day pass for traveling around the city and a two-day pass for exploring outside Amsterdam the next day. However, I was puzzled by his insistence that I should purchase my ticket ahead of them, and then he and his wife would purchase theirs. I couldn't quite grasp this habit, especially given that we were traveling internationally. I believed that it would be more logical for each of us to buy our tickets individually at separate counters, allowing us to choose the most convenient and comfortable approach for our purchases. Regrettably, due to his habit, I had already experienced a financial setback even before the trip started. Consequently, I refrained from making additional purchases under his influence. I must admit that I never openly addressed the unusual behaviour of my friend's husband, which tends to impose undue stress on others, resulting in both mental and financial challenges.

Tip: Avoid forcing your choices on others.

I also recall another incident before our trip when Annie and Peter would frequently conference call to discuss the itinerary, including air tickets, hotel bookings, and train tickets. During one of our discussions, we mutually agreed that one of the airlines offered most budget-friendly options. Oddly, Peter insisted that I take the initial step and make the booking first, assuring me that they would follow by booking their air tickets later. Witnessing his persistent nature to pressure people into booking first and promising to follow later not only makes you feel uneasy but also raises questions about whether there's a hidden agenda, such as a desire to pass on the potential loss or a potential change of plans.

Tip for individuals buying tickets separately but traveling as a group: Instead of insisting on a specific person booking first and others following, it's more appropriate to suggest choosing a particular option and buying individual tickets separately at different counters.

Tip for group ticket purchases: Choose a specific option and purchase tickets for everyone, then split the cost later.

Bus Journey

After getting a day pass, I asked the lady at the counter for directions to Nieuwe Kirke, a recommended spot for falafel. I was advised to take bus S Three Seven, but due to unclear pronunciation, I wasn't sure if it was S3 or S7. Peter led the way, but I remained convinced we were at the wrong spot. To confirm, I approached one of the bus drivers, who informed us we were on the wrong side of the road. After crossing over, we reached the correct bus stop. However, Peter insisted we follow him an extra 30 feet ahead where the bus driver suggested, and we followed him.

While waiting at the stop, I saw a bunch of people in military uniforms, so I asked a nearby lady to confirm. She checked the details on her phone and confirmed our bus was indeed waiting there, urged us to hurry before it left. It turned out to be the same stop the bus driver had mentioned before. Peter started running, and we followed, but I had to be careful due to my weak right knee. Despite often praising his sharp eyes, he couldn't spot the bus. When we reached the stop, the bus had already left. I shouted loudly, asking about buses numbered 3 or 7. Meanwhile, the bus had moved closer to the next stop, and same lady from the military group yelled that it was our bus. This made Peter sprint again, with Annie right behind him.

I attempted to run, but I realized I couldn't match Peter's pace. It wouldn't be fair if my health suffered from running, and I didn't expect others to take care of me or disrupt their trip. Unlike them, who had known connection in Europe, I made a point to prioritize my well-being and avoid overexerting myself.

I think it's important to take it easy when traveling. If you miss a bus, there are usually other options, so it's not a big deal to miss one.

During our train trip from Antwerp to Amsterdam earlier that day, Annie shared that she sometimes gets worried because of Peter's previous health issues. She was worried about his tendency to become overly excited in situations. Talking about the current situation of running after the bus, Annie said the bus number was S37, not 3 or 7. I clarified that I misunderstood because the lady mentioned digits, making me think they were two different bus numbers.

Tip: There's no harm in double-checking the bus number or confirming the right spot.

While running, Peter looked back at us instead of ahead, questioning why we asked others for confirmation when he had initially told us to wait at that specific spot. Such scolding can certainly ruin the mood. Sadly, because he was facing backward, he didn't see the pavement ahead, lost his balance, and fell, resulting in an injury. His hand got scratched, with some skin peeling and a bit of blood. Annie got emotional, tears welling up, which she held back. Peter quickly got up and directed us to board the bus.

He got on the bus first and we followed, Annie wondered if I felt like I was traveling with two older people. She brought up her near fall in Brussels and Peter's recent fall just five minutes ago. I reassured her that I wasn't thinking that way. However, as things unfolded in the next few weeks, it became clear that her statement unintentionally became true. I realized I was indeed traveling with more senior companions, a thought she had planted in my mind.

While Annie was still visibly upset, I attempted to lighten the mood and expressed my appreciation to Peter for his remarkable positivity that he had managed to set aside his own injury and remained determined to reach the attraction.

In the entire situation described above, if I hadn't asked the first driver, we met first, we would have wasted time. Furthermore, the bus driver and the military lady had indeed pointed us to the correct stop, and the one Peter directed us to was essentially the next one. However, it made me wonder, what if the bus had not stopped at the spot where Peter led us?

Peter should have shown maturity by realizing that causing an unnecessary commotion over not following his instructions could easily dampen the spirits of other travelers. During our bus journey, we had to change buses two times. To make sure we got off at the right stops and didn't waste time like before, I asked another passenger for confirmation. However, whenever Peter saw me talking to strangers, he would interrupt acting as if he didn't know much and monopolising all the guidance, seemingly with the goal of claiming credit for the entire day.

Finally, we reached Amsterdam Central and decided to try the highly recommended falafel. This time, they each got one falafel with shared French fries and juice. I bought a meal box for 13 euros, which had one falafel, one juice, and one portion of French fries. I added an extra euros for a 330 ml can of Coke. When Peter tried to grab my juice, I politely said I prefer not to share opened (sipped by me / others) drinks. Annie quickly clarified that their drinks were separate. Then Peter inquired about my can of Coke, and I explained I intended to have it later.

As we walked along the streets, we eventually reached the bridge. While on it, we took a moment to appreciate the view. There were canal boat rides with over 20 passengers and a private open boat. In the private boat, a man was accompanied by women dressed in revealing clothes, a sight that would undoubtedly grab anyone's attention.

Prior to the start of the trip, I proposed the idea of cycling in Amsterdam. Annie had refused, and Peter seemed interested. But when I asked a shop keeper about the cost (20 euros for an hour of cycling) in Amsterdam, Peter said we would do it later, hinting to postpone the activity after knowing the charges. Rather than allowing me to go cycling as planned, Peter delayed it with a promise of doing it "later" that never materialized. It would have been better if he had straightforwardly communicated his intention to save money and skip cycling. I could have gone on my own and met up with everyone later.

This showed he wasn't interested and preferred to skip the activity, indirectly expressing he'd rather not join. In my view, especially during an international trip, it's better to communicate directly. Clearly stating if you don't want to participate and suggesting others proceed without you, while planning to meet up later at a specific place and time, helps prevent misunderstandings and allows everyone to do what they prefer. On one occasion, I had already told them they could enjoy their tour to the windmill and cheese factory while we planned to meet at a certain spot at a specific time.

Heineken Museum

I had visited Amsterdam multiple times due to my work in aviation, so my goal was to discover new things in Amsterdam on this trip. When Annie and Peter suggested the Heineken Museum, I agreed. It was fascinating to see the inner workings of the beer factory and learn about Heineken's history. Upon entering, the staff provided us with wristbands for two free drinks each. But what started as an enjoyable experience turned unexpectedly uncomfortable because of inappropriate touch by my friend's husband, Peter, after consuming two glasses of beer.

The Heineken Museum is pretty big, and Annie usually walks briskly, while I move a bit slower because of my right knee and exercise extra caution on stairs. Annie rushed ahead on a staircase. Women tend to have an intuitive sense when something isn't right, and I had a similar feeling. I told Peter he should go down the stairs next instead of me. Surprisingly, he insisted I go first, following closely behind. Shockingly, he tapped his hand on the side of my hip. I was taken aback, bewildered by his actions, and unsure of his intentions. Women often have a sixth sense about touches being positive or negative. I briefly gave him the benefit of the doubt, thinking it might have been accidental.

When we reached another set of stairs, Annie was halfway down, and I once again asked Peter to go first. But he insisted I should go ahead. To my discomfort, he put his hand on my back briefly before taking it away. Suspecting he might be drunk, I decided to stay away. After the tour ended, we all assembled in a pub-like area in the Heineken Museum with loud music and unlimited complimentary beer. As Annie was tired we sat on one of the staircases.

Meanwhile, Peter spotted some people from his community who shared his regional language and struck up a conversation with them. I noticed that Peter displayed remarkable politeness towards strangers. He signalled for me to join, introduced me to the couple, and they suggested places like Lover's Canal, I'm ADAM, This is Holland, and few more. I listened to their suggestions and then politely left the conversation. The couple also told us about the prices for each attraction, like 16 euros for the Lover's Canal.

After they left, Peter suggested going to Lover's Canal. I mentioned that I had already taken a canal ride with my sister on previous trips and didn't desire another one. Despite my clear refusal, Peter persisted, repeatedly asking about the year of my previous canal ride. I found it perplexing that some people don't understand that "No" means "No." Surprisingly, Peter then offered to cover the cost of my canal ride, surprising both Annie and me.

I again politely declined, but he continued to insist on paying for the ticket. It left me pondering how someone who doesn't ensure his wife has proper meals, leading her to ask friends for items like Starbucks sandwiches, hotel croissants, or Coke, could offer to pay for my canal ride when I'm merely an outsider.

It reminded me of an earlier situation that day when the three of us witnessed a man in a boat with a couple of women. I wondered if his insistence was to boost his ego by being with two women. To conclude this conversation, I firmly suggested that he should go with his wife, Annie.

At Heineken, I made a thorough video of Annie and Peter's beer challenge, capturing everything from the beginning to the end. This way, they could choose to edit out any parts they didn't want.

Photos help keep memories alive. In my case, Annie recorded a video that began after I had already filled the glass with beer. Unfortunately, my face was partly hidden behind the tap. If she had moved a bit to the left, my face would have been in the video.

It's confusing that someone wouldn't think that a competition or event won't happen again. Common sense indicates the photographer should choose an angle that captures good video or pictures because we cherish these memories for a lifetime. It's sad that sometimes we have to remind people of common sense, but there's often little we can say to change their approach. I just kept my frustration to myself and didn't express my unhappiness.

On our way back from the museum, we waited at the bus stop to catch a ride back to the hotel. I noticed that during our conversation, Peter had positioned himself to my right and repeatedly tapped my shoulder while talking, all in the presence of Annie. Since Annie was on my left, to create more space, I intentionally shifted towards the other side of Annie, ensuring that Peter ended up on her right. Once we boarded the bus, I deliberately made an effort to sit away from him.

Sightseeing

The next day, we reached Central Station and went to the "I Love Adams" attraction, where you could swing in the air at a height. It was 5 minutes away from Central Station. Since only half of my beer challenge video at the Heineken Museum was recorded, I decided it might be better to ask strangers to take photos. When dealing with strangers, I don't mind if their photography skills aren't great. Sometimes, strangers even offer to take better photos themselves and ask if I'm happy with them. In those cases, I can ask them to retake the photo, and they usually understand. If I don't like the picture, I can easily find someone else to take a new one. The pictures taken by strangers at this attraction were good enough for me.

After we finished the attraction – I Love Adam's, we went downstairs and talked about what to do next. Peter wanted to visit windmills and a cheese factory, but since I had already done it twice on earlier trips, I wasn't interested. We agreed on a time to meet. Before leaving, Annie asked if I still had the Coke, which I bought at falafel shop. I was a bit puzzled as to why they were so curious about what I was eating, as this happened with my Starbucks sandwich, too. It felt like they were always keeping an eye on my meals and drinks. I explained that I had already consumed the Coke the previous night while talking to my mom.

What surprised me was that just the day before, Annie and her husband mentioned carrying some small cans of Coke from the event they attended in another European city. This left me more confused why they were asking about my drink when they already had some with them. Plus, we were at Central Station, so it wouldn't have been hard to buy more from a nearby grocery store. Throughout the trip, I stuck to my principles and didn't partake in their meals, so I wouldn't have been concerned about their food or drinks, even if they had them in front of me. Ultimately, I chose to overlook their questions.

I went to 'This is Holland' for a 5D view. It turned out to be a pleasant experience. I spent an hour there, enjoyed my snacks and coffee, and then watched the 5D show. It was a very peaceful and enjoyable experience.

THIS IS HOLLAND exclusively features the Netherlands, offering a comprehensive journey divided into four captivating parts. In just one hour, viewers are treated to the mesmerizing beauty of the "Low Countries." Through animated storytelling, the experience unfolds the narrative of a nation built below sea level, showcasing the unwavering determination of its people in overcoming this geographical challenge. The Dutch used different methods like windmills, mounds, dikes, and polders to take back land from the sea, making the Netherlands a unique country below sea level. The last of the tour includes being seated like you sit on an airplane, so you can buckle in and feel like you're flying over the Dutch scenery. With special effects, you get to see every part of the Netherlands in an exciting way, even if you can't visit all the tourist spots in just a few days. This amazing journey covers it all in just an hour, going beyond what you'd see on a regular tourist trip.

We agreed to meet near a store I was shopping. They called, stating they had reached the central location and would be at the store in 5 minutes. However, they arrived 20 minutes later, and Peter blamed Annie, mentioning her directions led them to the backside of the central area. I didn't voice any complaint about their lateness, and it didn't bother me much since I was busy exploring the streets and shops.

I thought it wasn't a big deal; sometimes you make wrong turns on a trip. During a leisure trip, trying different paths often gets you to the right one eventually. Their delay didn't bother me at all; I was busy shopping and really enjoying my personal time. So, I couldn't fathom why the husband was scolding his wife for it.

They were feeling fatigued, so we decided to take a short break at the hotel and get ready for our evening plans.

In the evening, I carried only one credit card and 10 euros with me knowing that we would be taking the night train to return to the hotel. We left the hotel at 9 PM to go to the central area. When we got there, they took me to see the Red-Light District. It was there that Annie revealed her husband wanted to visit the Red-Light District.

If she had informed me about her husband's interest in the Red-Light District beforehand, I would have chosen to stay in the hotel. Bringing a single girl to that area without warning felt indecent, and I wonder whether she would have made the same decision if it were her daughter in my position.

After our stroll, we selected a small, cosy restaurant for our meal. I asked about their food preferences, and we decided on pizza. I suggested ordering individually, but Peter insisted we share one pizza. The restaurant staff informed us that we needed to pay before getting our food, following the concept of paying first and then receiving your meal.

The bill was split evenly between the three of us, and I noted it in my daily expense records. We returned to the hotel by midnight.

Mugging of Laptop and Passport

The following day, our train to Zurich was scheduled for the evening, allowing for a 16-hour journey. To utilise our morning and afternoon time, we decided to explore the free market known as Albert Cuyp. We checked out of our hotel, deposited our luggage with the receptionist, and headed to the market. Surprisingly, it was right next to the Heineken Museum we visited two days ago. If we had known earlier, we would have visited on the same day we visited Heineken.

Around noon, they felt hungry, so I suggested going to McDonald's because I thought they might not prefer a fancier restaurant. While at McDonald's, Peter suggested getting 2 French fries and 1 McFlurry to share among three of us. However, I have a strong aversion to someone eating from my plate or using their used spoon in my ice cream, finding it unhygienic. It's different when someone takes a small portion of food from a communal platter onto their own plate, as there's no direct contact with their used utensils in my food. Therefore, I proposed that they order their own meal while I placed my own order. I sensed they were not thrilled that I wasn't sharing my meal. However, I prefer handling my own expenses for meals, shopping, tickets to any attraction or museums.

After coming back from the market, we freshened up in the lobby restroom, changed our clothes, grabbed our bags, and relaxed in the lobby. We still had few hours before going to the train station.

A week before our trip, Peter insisted on booking Swiss passes. He wanted me to book mine first, before they booked theirs. At that time, I preferred booking it closer to my actual days of arrival in Zurich. Once again, while seated in the lobby, he insisted I book first. I didn't understand why he always wanted me to book first, whether it was passes, meals, or hotels. I thought, since we were each paying for our own expenses, it didn't matter who booked first. I used the free time in the lobby to book my Swiss pass. Peter appeared relieved to know that I had finally booked mine and then proceeded to book theirs.

Our train ride was long, lasting 14 hours. Peter proposed we should reach the Central Station early, considering the 8:30 PM departure. In this case, Annie sought my permission to arrive an hour early, and I agreed. Whereas Annie didn't ask if I'd be comfortable going to the Red-Light District with her and her husband.

Peter, took the lead and got us to Amsterdam Central for our train to Zurich and Milan—like a whole hour and 20 minutes before departure time. Even though I noticed he often did the opposite of what's suggested, I stayed quiet and went along with them to avoid any possible blame.

When we left the hotel at 6:30 PM, we were all aware of the usual time it takes to reach the central station based on the last three days in Amsterdam. Although I believed we had ample time, he continued urging to leave early, worried about missing the train from Schiphol airport train station to central station. I thought that even if we missed one train from the airport, there would still be enough time for the next one. Arriving at the central station 30-45 minutes before departure would have been sufficient. However, due to his insistence, we went to the train station and arrived with an hour and 20 minutes to spare before the train departure time.

Peter suggested I check the inquiry counter for the platform details, and I asked Annie to watch my bags while I went. At the counter, I gave the train number, and they informed me that platforms are assigned 30 minutes before departure. As we were early, our train's platform hadn't been assigned yet, and I conveyed this information to Peter.

Tip: Remember that arriving too early at a train station can make you more vulnerable to potential dangers, as there might be people looking for chances to commit crimes like theft.

Theft doesn't always involve just one person; a group of possible wrongdoers might have been keeping a close eye on potential targets, especially since we were at the central station for over an hour. They would have seen that we had three suitcases, two pieces of hand luggage, and one laptop bag. In such a situation, anyone would think about what to target - the suitcases, the hand luggage, or the laptop bag. It's reasonable to assume that a smart thief would probably go for the laptop bag, as it often holds valuable and expensive items.

Another noteworthy incident occurred when we got to the platform. While checking the platform details on the TV screen, an unfamiliar person dark in complexion, shady looking, approached and stood behind Annie unexpectedly. I alerted Annie and recommended moving to a corner because this person's presence felt intimidating, but she didn't seem too worried, kept focusing on the TV screen for platform number, as if the situation didn't bother them.

The individual returned, looking like he was either searching for something or keeping an eye on something. When I suggested we move to sit on a nearby bench, they agreed. We found a bench near the staircase, sat down, and at that point, Peter became more at ease, almost carefree. He even placed the laptop bag on top of the large suitcase since we were all seated together.

There were a few other people around, maybe fellow travellers, I couldn't shake the feeling that thieves were keeping an eye on us.

Peter's impatience showed when the train, scheduled for 8:30 PM departure, arrived early at 8:00 PM, and he promptly urged us to board. Nevertheless, we still had a relaxed 30 minutes before departure, so there was no need to hurry. I wanted to emphasise that during this time, the train would be stationary, giving us enough time to locate our assigned carriage and seats and board when the crowd had thinned out.

Despite having 25 minutes before departure, Peter hurried without paying attention to the surroundings, urging us to board the train immediately. As more passengers joined, some approached the conductor on the platform to confirm train and carriage information.

While heading to the train, Annie diverged to the right, to talk to the train conductor in the opposite direction of her husband. I followed her, going the other way than Peter, each of us carrying our own bags. As Annie double-checked carriage details, Peter, realizing our separation or divergence, turned back and stationed himself exactly where the stairs led downward.

While Annie was trying to confirm the right carriage and train, her husband Peter, who often acted overconfident, didn't seem happy with her taking charge. Evoking a childlike demeanour, Peter energetically waved both hands aside from his luggage to grab Annie's attention. It was unnecessary since we were traveling together, and Annie had known him for over three decades; we would have recognized him instantly when we turned.

Releasing hold from the suitcase containing a laptop bag with a laptop and two passports, and waving both hands toward his wife, loudly shouting that he was showing the way to the carriage. Indeed, it was unusual for someone to release their luggage and wave like a child. As responsible adults, we would have sensibly returned to the spot where he was originally standing without the need for such behaviour.

It's likely that the person planning the theft was close to Peter. What probably caught the thief's eye was that Peter had secured the laptop strap by looping it around the luggage handle instead of wearing the laptop bag across his body, as he usually did. Unfortunately, his careless actions resulted in someone quickly taking the laptop bag within seconds, and he didn't realize the bag was gone.

He continued to scold his wife, stating he already showed her the carriage, so there was no need for her to confirm with the train conductor. Annie, visibly upset, hurriedly followed Peter onto the train, moving much faster than me. It seemed both were occupied - one scolding and the other being scolded - and unintentionally didn't even look back to check if I'm following behind. Consequently, they boarded and began arranging the bags without noticing if I had boarded the train or not. I was in line with other passengers to board and stayed vigilant about my surroundings. By the time I found my assigned seat, they had already arranged one of their bags in their designated spots. In the meantime, I secured a spot for my own bag in overhead compartment.

While this was happening, a man of Indian origin offered to help Peter to stow his bag in the overhead compartment. It was only then that Peter questioned if it was a first-class reservation, realizing the compartment had seats instead of sleepers. During the trip planning and reservation process much before the journey started, I attempted to convey to Peter the need for sleeper reservation which involved visiting the reservation desk and paying an extra 5 euros or more per person, while in that country, but he seemed uninterested. The realization of not listening to my initial advice struck him only upon seeing the coach for this 14-hour train journey.

Suddenly, he realized his laptop bag was missing. I told him I didn't know where it could be, and he started searching for it frantically, but couldn't find it. After looking thoroughly, it was sadly confirmed that they had fallen victim to theft.

Tip: You can buy many tracking gadgets that help you find your bag or passport if you lose them.

When I travel by train or plane, I always wear jeans with inside zipper pockets to keep my passport and cash safe. I examined my passport and felt relieved to find it safe and secure.

Peter hurried to check the platform for his laptop bag. I told Annie to stay with the bags and keep an eye on them while I joined Peter in looking. We went back to where the incident happened, and that's when I noticed he had been standing next to the staircase when the incident happened.

During one of the train journey to Amsterdam, I stressed the importance of avoiding staircases for a simple reason—they give potential thieves a chance to toss something onto the staircase. This allows an accomplice to quickly grab it and make a fast escape, disappearing from sight. Normally, victims are watching the people on the platform and don't notice the thief using the staircase to leave. However, even after I shared this, Peter overlooked it.

When Peter raised his hands in the air, the thief might have swiftly taken the laptop bag and discreetly put it on the staircase, allowing his accomplice to grab it and escape unnoticed. This would leave everyone looking for the bag without catching anyone.

When we couldn't find anything, Peter took the decision to disembark from the train. I, too, got off the train. I thought the older folks might struggle without passports, even though they had paid for hotels and trains. Peter suggested that I continue with the journey, and I saw my distressed friend Annie and without any hesitation, I said "Situations can happen to anyone, and we're in this together, so I won't leave."

Peter responded, "It's good you stay back as we might need your help and passport." He also pointed out that if I left, I'd keep worrying about their situation and how things would get sorted. That's when I noticed Peter not only mentioned the problem but also suggested a solution.

Out of the blue, Peter surprisingly said he would cover all the costs, a gesture that I found unexpected. I never thought about losing vacation time, missing hotel reservations, or feeling disappointed about not visiting places like Lake Como, Vatican City, and the major brand shops. My focus was on fixing the situation, not on the money I might lose.

Indeed, I had the choice to continue my journey, but I chose to stay with them in their tough time. I knew they might face problems at every step, my compassion led me to value friendship more than money.

At the train station, Peter consulted the train staff, and they advised going to the police station for assistance. As we left, Peter got upset, scolded Annie for asking the train conductor and me for following Annie. While Peter implied, I should have stayed with him to watch over his luggage, I disagreed because each of us had one bag and a handbag, and we were individually responsible for our belongings. Despite my differing opinion, I opted not to express it verbally.

Nobody told him to let go of his hands on bags and wave with both hands like a child. I stayed quiet but felt sorry for my friend having to take the blame for her husband's fault. My belief is simple: when things go wrong, focus on fixing the situation instead of blaming others, as you can't change the past.

I contacted my friend Nob in Canada, who works in aviation, to check if he had any connections in embassy. Despite not having any, he questioned why I didn't continue with my onward journey and let them manage the situation. However, when I expressed concern for their well-being, especially considering their age and my friend's husband's health issues, Nob realized my presence with them would provide emotional support to them.

I shared my worries with Nob, genuinely concerned about Peter's tendency to become highly stressed. The idea of how Annie would cope if something were to happen to him was constantly on my mind. It seemed impossible for me to leave someone in that situation.

Nob praised my decision, saying not many people would delay their own travels for others, especially after spending a lot on an international trip. Nob ended with, "I'm proud of you."

My friend Sophie called me in the morning after reading my messages about the incident. Her question mirrored the question asked by Nob - why I stayed back? I explained that I never contemplated leaving them in this situation, especially since they were elderly.

From the beginning of the journey, I sensed they wanted me along because I'm younger and could help and safeguard them in various circumstances. Sophie was impressed by my decision, saying not everyone would decide to change their own international plans for others.

Question to all Readers- what would you do in this situation?

We went to the police station to file a complaint. I asked Annie why they didn't keep their passports separate to avoid the stress of losing both. She admitted she asked her husband multiple times to hand her passport, but he always refused, displaying excessive confidence that he could handle things better. She also shared that he didn't like admitting mistakes and often blamed her for any mishaps.

I felt more at ease with my initial decision to follow whatever Peter suggested and be neutral, believing it would prevent him from blaming me for any issues during the trip.

I asked Annie about passport-sized photos, as I had given her a checklist before our trip. However, her response wasn't clear, leaving me uncertain whether she kept reminding Peter to take them but he didn't, or if the passport size pics were lost along with the laptop bag and passports.

At the police station, Peter filed the complaint, and I comforted Annie. Even though I'm not an expressive person, I strongly believe having someone with you in tough times is like finding shelter in a storm. They were relieved that the only loss was the laptop and passports. I suggested reporting any money loss because, if they claim insurance, it might help recover some money, factoring in any depreciation the travel insurance might consider for the lost items.

While Peter was in conversation with police, I realised that someone had to take proactive steps about our hotel and train bookings. Quickly, I sent a message to the Milan hotel, explaining the situation and asking for a free cancellation, even though our reservation was non-refundable. Because I knew about the hotel industry, I felt confident I could get a waiver. But when I shared this with Annie at the police station, her facial expression didn't show if she really understood what I said.

After obtaining the police report and necessary evidence for their safe return home, I advised Annie to make a copy of the report and send it to her son as a backup. The road from the police station to Amsterdam central was rough, causing damage to both front wheels of my baggage. Peter recommended I consider purchasing a new bag. Since we didn't have any hotel arrangements for the night, we searched for one near the police station, but they were expensive, around 600 euros per night for a single room. Luckily, one of their friends called and helped reserve two rooms at a hotel with a discounted rate. To go back to the hotel, we had to take the train from central to Schiphol airport.

Upon reaching the Amsterdam Central Station, Peter assumed that the thief might have thrown away the passports, and someone might have found and turned them in to the lost and found. Annie and Peter asked me to stay with the luggage at the center of the station while they looked for the lost and found department. I was a bit nervous being alone with three suitcases and two hand luggage pieces, but I knew Annie was worried about Peter's health and wanted to accompany him.

I was also conscious that Peter might blame me if something happened to their luggage. It was past 10 PM, and I realized opportunistic individuals might take advantage of our vulnerable situation. Knowing Peter's tendency to go against advice, which I noticed on the first day of our trip, I decided to stay alert. By now, I understood Peter's nature—he often ignores suggestions but pays more attention when money is involved. Therefore, I suggested going to the train station office which was 10 feet away to reschedule our tickets. This way, I could stay in a secure area while they went to the lost and found department. Peter agreed, saying, "Let's do that first, and then they can go find the lost and found." Unfortunately, the train station staff directed us to check on web application, the platform where we originally purchased our tickets.

It was unfortunate that we missed the train connection from Amsterdam to Zurich to Milan, especially since it was booked in first class—an idea I had suggested during the booking, believing first class was more suitable for longer train journeys, while second class was fine for shorter ones.

Normally, I book refundable tickets, but this time, most of our train tickets were booked together, and they chose the non-refundable, more economical option, resulting in the loss of the entire ticket cost. I had a similar experience with another ticket from Paris to Brussels, which was non-refundable. When I didn't board the night bus and onward train, the app only had a self-serve option for refunds, and it gave an automated response stating non-refundable tickets couldn't be refunded.

Tip: Opt for first-class on long train rides and choose second class for shorter trips.

Lost and Found

Peter and Annie decided to go to the lost and found, and I promised to wait near the ticket counter. Once they left, two heavy built guys showed up, acting like they were waiting in line but keeping a close eye on our bags.

I was conscious that if they overpowered me and took off with the luggage, Peter might blame me similar to how he blamed Annie for passport loss. So, I had to think fast and act quickly. I pretended to make a distressed call in English, stating that we had lost everything, including passports and money, and had nothing left. Surprisingly, they left within two minutes without asking anything at the desk. Isn't that a bit strange?

When Annie and Peter returned from the lost and found without success, I offered to contribute to the hotel stay. However, Peter insisted it wasn't my fault, and they would cover all the costs. Despite my insistence, he was firm, swearing on Annie, that he would cover all the expenses. Their gesture touched me deeply, and I held them in high regard for their kindness.

Return To Hotel

After finishing the hotel check-in, I accompanied them to their room for some comfort. Peter openly admitted that his carelessness was the only reason for the unfortunate incident. Annie also mentioned separately that her husband had admitted his careless mistake in front of the police.

Throughout this incident, there was a lack of clear leadership. Normally, a leader sets guidelines, and I usually stress the importance of having a designated meeting point if we get separated. Some have phones, some don't. In our group, Peter and I had phones, but Annie didn't have international calling. This raised concerns about how we'd contact each other if someone got separated. It was important to make sure everyone had access to money and credit cards. Unfortunately, there were no instructions about walking together and ensuring each other's safety because Peter wasn't inclined to give such guidance or take guidance from others.

Peter happily shared a story about a relative traveling with a large group who lost passport in another Schengen country. He proudly mentioned that the relative continued the journey to other countries after completing the necessary paperwork.

Even though I knew the relative could probably continue because others in the group had their passport IDs, which would have helped in case of any issues, I chose not to correct or tell Peter that his family member's travel journey went smoothly because others in the group were kind enough to support through their passports, thus avoiding any problems.

Usually, people complain about bad stuff to their friends but forget to talk about the good things others did for them.

Like Peter didn't appreciate the group that supported his relative when the passport was lost. Another time, in Brussels, when Annie lost her balance on an escalator, and I ran backwards to help her. She shared the escalator story with her relatives in Antwerp. They suggested she should have taken a taxi; she didn't mention that I ran backwards on the escalator to support her or that her husband was rushing her on the escalator. I thought, over time, we'll see how they'll treat me for supporting them when they lost their passport.

The risk is considerably reduced for travellers without a travel document when accompanied by someone who already has a passport and can vouch for them. Due to my experience in the aviation industry and awareness of rules and regulations that others might not, I chose not to correct or share these details. This was because they were still recovering from the mugging incident that happened a few hours ago. I stayed silent to avoid causing additional distress, knowing he might not easily accept different information. I also thought that his relative's experience of traveling to other Schengen countries after losing their passport serves as encouragement for him, making him believe he could do the same. I supported his motivation to continue without any hindrance.

Unexpectedly, Peter admitted that the situation was a result of carelessness and left a message on his laptop for the thief, requesting to return the passports. A little while later, he used his phone to erase all the data on his laptop. We decided to meet at the breakfast table the next morning since we planned to visit the Indian embassy in Amsterdam. After making sure they were both comfortable, I intentionally placed the Indian food pack that Annie gave me in Brussels on a side table to ease their worries about meal expenses during the trip before heading to my room.

By the time I settled in my room, it was 4 AM in India, and I couldn't contact anyone for help; I chose to wait until morning to use my connections. I called my mother, explained the entire situation, and requested her to pray that nothing else goes wrong.

Tip: Call your loved ones; even a simple call to your family, especially mom or sibling, can have its benefits akin to receiving a hug. Simply hearing her voice can help reduce the stress levels of your trip.

The next morning, I contacted my former senior colleague, a retired person who held a high-ranking position at the airport, known for his influential network and problem-solving skills. I hold great admiration and respect for my ex-colleague because of his unwavering positivity and willingness to help others. He's a compassionate and reliable individual who always encourages others to be their best. One of my favourite bosses, and I'm genuinely thankful for his friendship. I explained the unusual situation and asked if they could provide guidance or support in obtaining the necessary documentation, like the white passport, to help them return home. My senior colleague gave me a contact name, Andrew, at the Indian embassy in Amsterdam.

During breakfast at the hotel, Peter suggested not informing the embassy in Amsterdam about their return flight from Zurich to avoid complications. Personally, I think it's better to share all information with the embassy as they are there to help during challenging situations, and withholding details might complicate matters. With my background in the aviation industry, I strongly felt that if they risked boarding a flight from Switzerland with a travel document issued in the Netherlands might lead to denial boarding since one usually has to exit from the country that issues the document.

I stayed quiet because I understood Peter disliked taking advice, especially since he strongly believed his relative could travel without a passport, so he could do the same. Another reason for my silence was the worry that if things didn't go as he hoped, he might entirely blame me. So, I chose to keep quiet and planned to ask Andrew directly to avoid being held responsible for any possible problems.

We checked out of the hotel and met Annie's acquaintances at a planned spot. On the bus, I comforted my friend Annie, reassuring her things would get sorted, and I'd be there for them during the rest of the trip. It was heartening to see her smile. I also said I had taken leave for almost a month and couldn't extend my trip beyond Zurich if any flight issues occurred. Our return flights were different but departing from the same airport. I explained that I would offer all the help possible, but changing or cancelling my flight wouldn't be feasible because of work obligations. She understood and was okay with it.

Annie's acquaintances who stayed in Amsterdam were familiar with the ways and surroundings, they walked us to the entrance of the Indian embassy but couldn't come inside with us. They intended to meet us after our visit. We rang the embassy's doorbell, and a casually dressed individual came out, asking the purpose of visit. Peter explained the situation regarding the lost passports and laptop, and the security personnel asked further questions while Peter continued to provide the necessary details.

After a while, I asked the officer if Andrew was available and mentioned my reference from my ex-colleague. Until then, I hadn't informed Annie and Peter about my embassy connection. Their expressions changed, showing relief, and they became hopeful upon realising we might get assistance.

Prior to escorting me to Andrew, the officer told Annie and Peter to go to the counselor's office. When I met Andrew, I introduced myself, mentioned the reference, and explained the whole situation, asking for guidance on the next steps. He assured me he was ready to help.

Andrew led me into the embassy, and I was amazed by its beauty, featuring spacious seating areas and wall paintings. He inquired about my friends, noticing their absence. I explained that they had gone to the counsellor's office through the outer gate. When Annie and Peter returned, looking serious and disappointed, I introduced them to Andrew and asked the details of their meeting. Peter shared the counsellor's advice, which included filling out an online form, getting passport-sized photos, and paying embassy fees before getting an emergency certificate (EC) for the next day. An EC is a one-way travel document valid only for the return trip to the home country and is issued after the High Commission is satisfied with the bona-fides of the applicant. I won't specify the exact fees, as they can vary for travellers who lose passports after few years from now.

I asked Andrew if he could check with the counsellor about this situation. While Andrew went to inquire, I comforted Annie, assuring her not to worry as Andrew would help. This sparked Peter's enthusiasm, and he began suggesting that we provide more details to Andrew, including their UK and USA visas and past international travels. He continued explaining in detail.

I asked Annie if I could handle the interaction on my own since it was my contact, and my senior colleague had given the reference. Given Peter's behaviour over the past eight days, I worried that any feedback from the embassy to my senior colleague could reflect poorly on me. Annie understood my concern and suggested to Peter to be patient and he let me take care of the situation.

When Andrew returned, he explained that they had to fill out online applications. After getting their Emergency exit certificates, they should quickly book tickets from Amsterdam and immediately leave the country. He emphasised not to make any more travel plans. Embassies usually give documents with specific instructions, similar to visa issuance. For example, a Schengen visa from the French embassy might be valid for two years, while one from the Spanish embassy could cover 30 days of travel. The Austrian embassy might issue a visa for the exact days of your planned trip.

I understood from Andrew that once they received the emergency exit certificate, they couldn't stay in the country and had to leave the next day. Despite Peter's desire to continue their journey, Andrew emphasized the risk of traveling without passports on the onward journey. It was disheartening for all of us.

I checked with Andrew if Annie and Peter could travel to Italy, Belgium, and Switzerland by purchasing new air tickets and showing a police report in lieu of their lost passports. He recommended taking the train as the safest option, as immigration authorities might not allow them on a flight, creating more issues. I also inquired about their valid visas connected to the lost passports. He clarified that these visas would be voided along with the cancelled passports, requiring new visas.

I shared with Andrew in confidence that Annie and Peter didn't inform the counsellor about their return flight from Zurich. I questioned if this could affect their return journey. He said that he will check and confirm. I mentioned that booking new flights from Amsterdam would be expensive. Andrew confirmed that the cost wouldn't be less than 2 lakhs for one way return ticket for one person. Peter chimed in that It's a huge cost to them.

I understood Peter's concerns and didn't want them to face significant losses. I suggested alternatives to Andrew, offering my passport to accompany them and inquired about flying to Rome. Andrew clarified that international flights without passports were not feasible, recommending road or train travel instead.

All countries insist on having a passport for international flights; photo IDs or other forms of identification won't suffice. Andrew suggested completing the forms online and getting passport-sized photos, and he would consult with the counsellor again. Andrew mentioned that he wasn't originally supposed to be at the embassy that day, but his plans changed at the last minute, so we were fortunate to find him there. We thanked him and left the embassy.

While waiting for Annie's acquaintances, Andrew called and suggested we visit the Embassy of India in Berne, Switzerland for a white passport. This would enable the couple to return home and use their return tickets. I thanked Andrew and mentioned that I would let the couple make the decision and confirm shortly. Annie's acquaintances arrived, and Peter explained the situation to them in his regional language.

Andrew called again to check if Annie and Peter were bringing the required photos, as he had kept the counsellor past regular hours. I quickly checked with Peter about their decision and relayed that the couple would go to Berne for the necessary documentation instead of returning to the embassy. I expressed my sincere gratitude to Andrew for his efforts and the counsellor for staying late to help. Note that the embassy issuing the emergency certificate or white passport will also cancel the lost passports.

Tip: When holding an emergency certificate, make sure to catch your departing flight from the country that issued the certificate.

After obtaining passport-sized photos and paying 17 euros per person, which included only four photos each, we proceeded to their acquaintance's house. The house was filled with five adults and two kids beside the three of us. Peter used his acquaintance's laptop to fill out the online application. I observed that he liked doing things on his own, so I didn't offer help with the application. Even his acquaintances didn't interfere while he was filling out the form.

Tip: It's advisable to keep eight passport-sized photos with you at all times. This alleviates concerns in case of passport misplacement or the need for photos, as obtaining them abroad can often be more expensive, often costing 15 times more in euros or dollars compared to obtaining them in your own country.

Annie got busy chatting with other ladies. Feeling excluded as everyone spoke in their regional languages, which I couldn't understand, I decided to use the time to express my gratitude to my senior colleague in India and shared a detailed update on my interaction with Andrew.

My senior colleague praised me for my wise decision that I shared the return flight from Zurich with Andrew, ensuring proper guidance and avoiding a situation where they would need to return home country within 48 hours. My senior colleague also highlighted that if the embassy had issued the emergency certificate and they proceeded with their onward journey in Europe, they would have faced boarding denial in Zurich. Then, forced to return to Amsterdam, buy new return tickets and then depart from Netherlands, incurring additional expenses. Thanks to my quick thinking, we were able to avoid unnecessary trouble. Moreover, if Annie and Peter had been caught traveling in Europe with the emergency certificate and not departed from country, it could have led to more problems, like legal consequences for staying in a country without a valid permit or visa, as their previous passport and visa would have become void.

Although my senior colleague appreciated my actions, Annie and Peter didn't express any gratitude or acknowledgment, neither for my support nor for connecting them with the embassy contact, ultimately saving them money and time during their journey.

Tip: Always be honest with the embassy. It can make your life easier in a foreign country. They are your main support if you're alone.

The ladies at home cooked yummy food. Annie and I ate first. I thanked Annie's acquaintances for the tasty lunch and chatted with an older uncle there.

Peter submitted both applications online, believing they were going to the Berne embassy. However, it turned out he submitted his application to the Berne embassy and Annie's to the Geneva embassy, which we discovered when we reached the embassy.

It was quite surprising to see Peter, who often considered himself intellectually superior to his wife, made such an error in filing a passport application. Quite unusual!

Peter closed the laptop and joined others for lunch. Cleverly, he asked me to book train tickets from Amsterdam to Berne. I used a train app, shared the cost, and Annie handed me Peter's card. To buy the tickets, I had to remove my saved card details and use his, but I declined. I prefer keeping financial transactions with friends clean. Aware that Peter tends to blame others, I worried he might hold me responsible if something went wrong with his card later. So, I politely said no to Annie, insisting only my card details should be on my app.

It was odd that Peter, who usually jumps into talks, stayed quiet this time. He enjoys taking control, so why didn't he handle booking the train? What's the harm in waiting until he finishes his meal?

Strangely, whenever there was a financial transaction, he always asked me for assistance, and I couldn't understand why. If Peter wanted, he could've used his phone to book with his cards after lunch.

Even an older uncle there insisted me to book. Feeling pressured and cornered amongst 10 people known to Annie and Peter, I booked the tickets. By the trip's end, it was clear Peter was focused on money matters.

It was strange that when eating with family, they happily had big meals, but when paying for themselves, they chose to split the meal.

We returned to the hotel, and Peter decided to print a few copies of reservations as they had lost the itinerary with the laptop bag. I told Annie I only had a printout of my train ticket to Lucerne and suggested printing their tickets too. I also proposed printing the rest of our plans, but Peter was concerned about how the hotel staff might see it, so he wanted to keep the copies limited. It was clear again that he had a specific way of doing things, so I didn't suggest anything more. Having worked in hotels, I knew most don't charge for printouts, and those that do usually direct guests to a business centre where fees might apply. I didn't understand why he hesitated to get their documents printed. Maybe it was because I made the suggestion, and he tended to do the opposite. So, I decided to use my time wisely and called my friends and family.

After a while, I craved for coffee, so I asked Annie if she wanted some, but she declined, Peter, however, wanted a cappuccino. I ordered a cappuccino, which is usually served in a small size, and a latte for myself, typically presented in a larger glass. Carrying the coffee tray, I thought Peter might like the latte more because it's larger. So, I left the tray near the printer desk, told him one was a cappuccino, and the other was a latte. I gave him space to choose while I stepped away to make a call. He picked the bigger latte mug just to boost his ego.

I was happy that my guess was right when he picked the latte, which is indeed bigger. I rejoined and enjoyed my cappuccino. After he finished the latte, he expressed dissatisfaction, saying it was too milky and not to his liking. The lesson here is that when people change their usual preferences of food and drinks, it doesn't mean they'll enjoy it. I found his reaction funny and decided not to worry about it. Personally, I like both cappuccinos and lattes, so it didn't matter much to me.

The recently booked tickets were for the train journey from Amsterdam to Basel, one stop before Zurich. Everything, including the train and platform, remained unchanged from the previous day. As we reached platform, a mix of emotions arose. The train arrived at 8:00 PM, and for the first time, we jointly decided to let others board first because we had over 20 minutes before departure.

Personally, I was more vigilant, closely observing the passengers to spot any potential thieves. While waiting on the platform, Annie complained about traveling with big suitcase and expressed in frustration to get rid of it. I shared my practice of storing bags at Schiphol Airport after a few days of travel, opting to carry only essentials I needed in a small bag for the rest of the trip. Additionally, I mentioned regretting not booking my return flight from Amsterdam, which would have made it easier to store my luggage at the airport for a few days and picking it up before going home.

I highlighted the convenience of storing bags in lockers, it lets you move around hands-free. Peter, however, remained silent, not adding to the conversation. When people discuss different topics, their level of participation often reveals where their interests or priorities lie. In this instance, it was clear that Peter had no interest in spending money on lockers.

I suddenly noticed a guy in a red t-shirt and shorts. He didn't have anything with him, he was without any luggage or handbag, totally empty handed and seemed to be watching people closely. Our eyes met briefly, and it seemed like he might not have good intentions. He then shifted his attention to other passengers and boarded the train from the adjacent carriage. We also entered the train and prepared for a 12-hour journey.

Approximately 20 minutes after the train left the platform, I noticed another person walked by, followed by the guy in the red shirt, seemingly accompanied by another person. The second person took a window seat three rows ahead of us, while the other two walked to the next compartment.

None of them had any luggage or carried anything. I whispered to Annie that the guy in the red shirt from the platform was now on the train and seemed to have suspicious intentions, possibly related to theft. I couldn't shake the thought that he might be the one who stole Peter's laptop bag. Then, surprisingly, I observed the man seated by the window seat moved to the same compartment as the guy in the red shirt. In less than 10 minutes, I witnessed the man in the red shirt returning to our compartment with a red and black stroller and a small duffle bag. Once again, our eyes met, and I was certain he knew I recognized him as a thief. After our brief exchange of glances, he left for the other compartment.

Witnessing another theft was disheartening, and the thought of yelling to warn everyone crossed my mind. However, I hesitated, mindful that thieves often operate in groups. I didn't want to shout because his friends might be in the same or nearby carriage, and it could be risky for me. Worried about my safety, I chose to stay quiet. I felt sad for the traveller who suffered the loss.

About an hour later, at the next station, the guy in the red shirt left with the bags.

In European and international trains, there are specific spots for putting luggage. These storage areas can be found at the front and rear of each compartment, primarily meant for storing larger or bulkier luggage. Smaller luggage can typically be stowed in the overhead compartment or under the seat.

From what I saw and heard lately, it appears that thieves often target people with smaller bags, such as duffle bags or laptop bags. These bags are easy to steal, and the thieves can get away quickly. This is especially risky for older travellers who might struggle to keep up with the pace of a thief.

Tip: Opt for luggage that fits under your seat during night time train trips to easily notice if anyone attempts to take it. Avoid bringing a small stroller, as it could be a target for theft.

During this and upcoming train journeys I always reminded them to keep a close watch on their bags stowed in the rear of the train compartment - that was my way of showing concern towards them.

Annie brought homemade bread with a shelf life of up to 20 days. She opened the same box I had left on a side table of her room previous night. Annie generously offered either homemade bread or Indian snacks (bhujias). Despite not being particularly fond of Indian food or snacks, her kindness prompted me to take a piece of bread, especially considering there weren't any other food options on the train.

Locker

Annie joined Peter in the back seat, and their discussion about taking their bags to the embassy indicated that they didn't plan on using lockers. Despite previously sharing information about locker facilities in Europe, I considered avoiding the topic at our next stop in Basel because Peter tends to ignore advise. Instead, I opted for my usual European travel approach—leaving luggage at the train station or airport and carrying only a light shoulder bag with essentials. Concerned, I thought of asking the railway station attendant about locker facilities. Anticipating Peter's inclination to copy others, I expected his regular response would be: "I'll keep mine too; why should we be left behind?"

We reached Basel for our transfer to Berne—a one-hour ride. While trying to find the platform for the train to Berne and checking locker availability, I asked a representative, "What's the platform number for the train to Berne, and is there a locker facility to store my bag?" In a typical Peter style, he chimed in, questioned my decision to store only my bag and not theirs. In response, I conveyed that "I wasn't certain about your willingness to spend on such conveniences as you often preferred carrying luggage everywhere"

This further confirmed the observation that he often mirrors the actions and choices of others, whether it's related to food, drink preferences or decisions like using lockers. if I get sandwiches, he does too; if I have coffee, he goes for beer; if I have curd, he follows to buy, if I want to store my bag in locker, he wants it too. His behaviour often resembled that of a copycat.

This pattern of behaviour occurred repeatedly 1) copying me 2) doing the opposite of suggestions 3) replicating my actions when I don't ask. I suggested using a locker on the night train to Annie based on my preference for day trips and a dislike for the constant burden of carrying luggage, preferring a hands-free approach to travel. However, there wasn't much response. On the contrary, they discussed carrying their luggage to the embassy. I also recalled Peter's remark during my day trip to Bruges that he likes carrying luggage, checking into the hotel, and then doing sightseeing. This corresponds with our previous night's discussion when he expressed a liking for carrying luggage. In contrast, I preferred going to the embassy without heavy bags, wanting a hands-free approach.

Ultimately, he suggested storing our bags, assuring he would cover all expenses until we reached Rome, our next destination, and from there, the actual financial arrangements would begin. He took responsibility for the loss caused by his action. He secured a large locker, and put our luggage, including mine, inside. Only then did he realize the convenience of moving around freely and comfortably to the embassy without the burden of heavy bags.

Furthermore, I found it puzzling that they happily travelled by train throughout our trip and seldom took taxis. So, when it came to taking the underground train from the hotel to Brussels Midi on day two, I couldn't understand why they raised objections at that time. It appeared to me that they cared more about saving money over convenience and comfort.

Way to Embassy

The Swiss passes we got online in Amsterdam were really handy. We didn't need to bother with buying tickets every time; we could hop on trams, buses, boats, and trains with unlimited access for the purchased days. Plus, it came with discounts for various attractions.

In Berne, the passes made it easy to take the tram and find the embassy, which was close to the train station, only two tram stops away and a short 6-minute walk. Annie walked ahead, I was behind her, and Peter was behind me. Out of nowhere, he touched my back, which startled me and I screamed. Annie turned to ask but Peter said nothing happened. We crossed the road and reached the embassy gates.

Peter pressed the doorbell, and when asked about our visit through the speakerphone. Peter started explaining our long journey from the beginning, mentioning our stops like Amsterdam. Growing impatient, I interrupted, saying, "Hey, we've lost our passports!" That was the main issue. Surprisingly, someone quickly opened the door. However, Peter started yelling, saying, "Let me talk, I'm speaking," in a not-so-polite way. I didn't like the tone, so I stepped back and allowed him to handle the situation as he saw fit.

I questioned Annie about Peter's rude behaviour. She clarified that she had requested him several times to give back her passport, but he refused, saying he'd keep it safe. Annie continued to reveal that she felt pressured because she'd be blamed if she lost items, and even if Peter lost them, the blame would still fall on her. She was hurt and worried. We made ourselves comfortable on the sofas and let Peter interact with the counsellor independently.

After speaking with the counsellor, Peter shared that the counsellor identified an error in his form. He admitted that he made a mistake in the form. He filled out his form correctly, but he accidentally filled out Annie's form for the Geneva embassy. This made us wonder if he actually planned to go to Geneva now. Realising his mistake, he requested the counsellor to accept Annie's application. The counsellor was accommodating and told him to fill out a new application. She instructed him to send Annie's application in PDF format through email. We still had 11 days left on our trip at that point. Furthermore, the counsellor made it clear that the police report from the Netherlands would not be accepted, and they must file a new police report in Switzerland to get the passport. The passport-issuing government only considers reports from their own country.

Tip: To get the new temporary passport, you need to give the police report from the country issuing the passport. Police Reports from other countries won't be accepted for this purpose.

On the way to the police station, Annie mentioned the need to grab a meal and suggested to tell Peter. The last proper meal we had was at their acquaintance's house the day before, so it had been almost 24 hours without a full meal. I sensed that Annie was sharing this concern to me but perhaps hesitant to ask her husband to buy a meal. In response, I proposed to Peter that after finishing their police stuff, we should grab brunch since it was almost noon. Peter happily agreed, saying, "Yes, that's a great idea!" Peter's unpredictability always amused me, considering his initial hesitation regarding spending on a meal, but now he seemed quite eager to eat.

Typically, family members vent their stress and anger with each other rather than with strangers. This might make one partner feel silent and seek help from strangers instead, asking them to make a request to their family as if it's their own to avoid being scolded. Annie found herself in a similar situation.

The government of Switzerland charges a fee for re issuance of any document. In their case, Police charged a fee for filing a fresh report of passport theft. Once they handed the report, we returned to the embassy again to submit the police report for further processing. Peter decided to apply for an emergency passport which is limited to one year or less and doesn't have an embedded electronic chip.

On our way back, we stopped at Starbucks, Peter asked what I wanted to eat, and I knew they were paying. I didn't want to make things too expensive for them, so I picked something affordable – a simple yogurt with crunchies and strawberries on top. Even though I had the option to go for a sandwich higher pricier item, I purposely went for the cheaper option.

Excitedly, Peter chose the same sandwich I got at the Starbucks in Antwerp station when our journey began. As a gesture of courtesy, I offered them a taste of my small portion of curd. They both tried it and liked it. That's when Peter mentioned they lost their travel adapter during the laptop incident. In response, I shared my travel adapter and an Apple cord, despite its somewhat damaged condition. I only requested that they handle it with care when plugging and unplugging it from their devices.

During the trip, I prioritized their mobile charging needs. I always let them charge their phones and Apple Watch first, in case they needed to make calls and feel comfortable. This was my main concern for them. I typically charged my phone last after making sure their devices were fully charged.

As we discussed our upcoming trip from Milan to Rome, we realized we had already missed today's train from Milan since we were currently in Berne. In response, Peter instructed me to check various train apps to find the fastest way to reach Rome. Upon using a mobile app for train reservations, I discovered it would cost 750 euros for three people. Politely, I asked if it was alright for me to go to the train reservation counter at the station to book the tickets in person. I explained that in my previous trips to Europe, I always liked direct counter booking.

My patience had worn thin with how he spoke to me at the embassy. So, I subtly hinted that he should continue charging his phone and take some time to relax since he seemed stressed. Annie and I would handle the ticket booking. He liked the idea and said, "Sure, go ahead." At the train counter, the attendant told me there were no available trains to our destination due to road construction. But I insisted and asked her to check for alternative routes. Eventually, she found one connection with a quoted price of 700 euros for three people. I asked about any discounts or promotions. The attendant asked if we had a Swiss pass, which could get us a discount. Even though my Swiss pass was supposed to activate after 6 days, she still gave us a 50% discount. This reduced the final price to 350 euros.

Tip 1: If you have a Swiss Pass while traveling in Europe, it's better to avoid booking advance train tickets to other countries through various mobile apps. These apps usually don't give the 50% discount that the Swiss Pass offers. The Swiss Pass grants a 50% discount when you buy train tickets at Swiss train stations for travel to other countries, making it generally a more cost-effective option to buy tickets at the station.

Tip 2: For travellers to Europe with a Swiss Pass: Booking train tickets to other countries at Swiss train stations can take advantage of the 50% discount, a cost-effective choice. Always double-check the specific terms and conditions of your Swiss Pass and your planned routes, as policies may change over time.

Tip 3: Sometimes, it's better to buy train tickets at the counter instead of online, especially when there are issues like road construction. Counter staff can offer better route options to deal with such situations compared to booking online.

I also asked if we could get sleeper beds for the night train. The staff mentioned it would cost an extra 5 euros per person, and I agreed. I waited patiently for Annie to pay for the train tickets but had a feeling she didn't have her credit card. I asked if we should go ahead with the booking since we had a good discount but she replied that she needed to consult with Peter. We only had an hour to get our bags from locker and freshen up before catching the train from Berne station and I realized neither Annie had a card nor the funds. Ultimately, I ended up using my credit card by default, as going downstairs to consult with Peter for approval and re-joining the queue would have consumed too much time, risking us missing our connection.

In my opinion, if Peter's approval was necessary, he should have been either been present at the booking counter or given his credit card to his wife beforehand. Going back to the counter would have involved waiting in line again, finding the next available representative, and going through the entire process of selecting train options, calculating fares, and applying discounts from the start. This could have wasted a lot of time and posed the risk of missing our connection.

This situation indicated two things:

a) His wife might not have had access to money or a credit card.

b) It seemed like Peter wanted to use my credit card without directly asking me, possibly as part of his strategic plan. This could involve making me incur higher conversion fees because his card required daily top-ups via international calls to his team, ensuring that the card had the daily minimum balance. He might have been taking advantage of a more favorable conversion rate through his contacts but chose not to reveal the exchange rate.

c) Before the trip, Peter refused to tell me the exchange rate he got for the currency. It was only later during the journey that I figured out he intended to make a profit from it.

It's ironic that he promised to cover expenses, but in reality, he was making me spend more due to the additional conversion costs.

Later in the trip, I discovered his plan to balance the 600 euros I spent on all the train bookings until now by covering some of my expenses, like bus or museum tickets, using his card. However, I didn't have any plans to spend that much in such a short time. While his idea was smart, it also showed a bit of selfishness on his part.

Tip: Group travellers should consider everyone's preferences and communicate openly to avoid misunderstanding and causing offense unintentionally.

After buying the train tickets, we returned to Starbucks. I was surprised to see Peter enjoying the same yogurt I had just an hour ago. It was even more surprising because Annie and Peter had been splitting every meal, so I couldn't understand why he didn't do the same this time or ask if Annie wanted anything or if she was hungry.

He began with a dramatic expression, claiming that he was worried about both of us and thought we were lost. I found it amusing since he had been casually wandering around the cafe, enjoying his yogurt, a sight witnessed by both Annie and me. His fake concern seemed unnecessary, especially since he didn't ask if I wanted another yogurt, though I could handle my expenses. What surprised me even more was his lack of concern and courtesy towards his wife. It seemed like he never considered her needs, showing insensitivity by not offering her food or ordering something similar for her. Temporarily, I excluded myself from the equation as I can independently meet my needs. I reasoned that I shouldn't interfere in a couple's relationship; it's their life and their way of living. If he chooses to continue showing indifference or a lack of affection towards her, there's little I can do.

While traveling from Bern to Rome, we switched trains three times. At one station, where Annie and Peter climbed stairs with their bags, a young man in his twenties spontaneously offered help by grabbing one of my bag straps as we ascended. He suggested I let go, but my instinct told me to maintain a tight grip on my bag, so we ascended together.

Upon reaching the platform, he hastily boarded the right side of the train just before the doors closed. This made me recognize the potential risk – imagining the scenario, where, had he been a thief and I had let go of my bag, I wouldn't have had sufficient time to catch up with his pace and he could have easily run away with my bag.

My caution came from noticing his quick pace and stories of people pretending to help while intending to steal. It's crucial to stay alert in such situations. As we continued our train journey to Rome, Annie suggested Peter take a short nap to rest. While he slept, Annie and I chatted casually. Peter was always alert to conversations about him, often waking up when Annie and I mentioned his name. I jokingly called his attentiveness a "hawk's view." Ironically, despite his sharp awareness, he couldn't prevent the loss of his laptop bag and passport.

After two hours, we arrived at a small station with two platforms. Finding the next train an hour away, I suggested using a secure waiting area with glass doors and windows providing clear visibility of anyone entering the room. Annie and I settled in, and Peter later informed us that we needed to go beneath the platform to reach platform 2.

The station, resembling those in villages, was notably small with no elevator. Going down the stairs with our bags was manageable, but climbing up was exhausting, especially for Peter, who had to assist Annie with her luggage first. An Italian gentleman kindly approached and offered help to Peter and me. This time, I was fine with this middle aged gentleman carrying the suitcase to the platform without me holding the bag, as Annie and Peter were already awaiting at the platform, facing the staircase. We expressed our gratitude to him. This was the second time I noticed Peter's remarkable politeness towards strangers.

After few hours, we reached another station where we needed to switch trains again. This platform was convenient for dragging our luggage. The next train to Rome was scheduled to depart in an hour, so we settled in for a wait. As time passed, a few more passengers joined us. This was a night train journey.

At each station, I chose not to ask Annie's husband for help with my bag, preferring to do things independently. Their main focus seemed to be on organizing themselves and their luggage, regardless of whether I had boarded the train or not. On the day they lost their laptop bag in Amsterdam, heading to the center of the compartment where our seats were, and promptly arranging their bags, while I arrived later, displayed insensitivity, a lack of consideration, and did not constitute a protective gesture at all. In fact, at many stops, it was the passengers behind me who took the initiative to lift my bags and place them near the train doorway. I appreciate his proactive assistance in lifting the bag and stowing it in the overhead compartment inside the train on several other occasions. However, for safety, it would have been appropriate to say, "After Annie, you board the train," or "I (Rebecca) board first, followed by Annie," to confirm if I had indeed boarded.

On this night train to Rome, we had sleeper class, and they were pleased to find our room within the train compartment. There were six rooms, each with three beds stacked one above the other. A complimentary box with towels and slippers was provided on each berth, and water cans were placed next to the washbasin for our convenience. I asked them which bed they would prefer since I was mainly interested in getting some rest to wake up at 5 am. The train journey was a lengthy 9 hours, and a good night's sleep was crucial for me to be ready to visit the next day's attractions. Annie decided the bottom berth, and suggested Peter take the middle one, leaving the top berth for me. I continued to be accommodating and refrained from expressing that I should take the top berth simply because I was younger than them. Out of consideration for their age, I chose not to voice any concerns.

The room was small, and with both Annie and Peter inside, there wasn't enough space for me to climb to the top berth unless they both moved out or one of them sat on the bottom berth while the other stepped out. I couldn't understand why Peter was so focused on inspecting the complimentary items instead of giving me some space to climb up. Eventually, Annie must have noticed my impatience, so she urged Peter to step out of the room, allowing me to climb to the top berth. Within a few minutes, I had fallen asleep.

We woke up to a knock on the door, and the train host delivered coffee shots. These shots are meant to give us a quick energy boost. My coffee shot was good and suited my taste, but Annie found hers bitter because of the limited amount of milk. Trying to help, I asked the train representative for two shots, one for me and one for her. I handed the coffee shot to her, but it seemed she hadn't quite developed a liking for the strong taste of shots.

Don't regret traveling; every experience makes your future trips even better.

Chapter 5

Unexpected Encounters: Navigating Uncertainty in Rome

We got off the train in Rome at 5:30 AM and opted for a taxi to our hotel because it was quite far in an industrial area from the city centre. It was a decent hotel. When we reached the hotel, I suggested they stay seated while I managed the check-in process since hotels need your passport for check-in.

When the receptionist asked for the passport details, I informed her that my friends lost their passports but I could provide her with the police report. She explained that they typically require the actual passport for identification and wouldn't allow check-in without it. I requested if she could make an exception and use only my passport. She agreed, scanned my passport, and said check-in was after 2 PM. I mentioned our check-in was for yesterday, but we couldn't reach due to the mugging incident. I also mentioned we should get our complimentary breakfast. Realizing the mistake, she gave us the room keys. As a habit, I asked the receptionist to give me the name, address, and phone number of the hotel in their native language so that I could keep it in my purse for easy access. Peter displayed his eagerness to go sightseeing. He wanted to stay on schedule even if it meant we couldn't rest enough.

Tip: Take the business card of the hotel.

I suggested I'd have breakfast while they got ready. I kind of hinted that since the three of us share the room, the guy could have breakfast while Annie and I freshen up. But Annie said Peter had to bring the bags to the room. I said, "I'm going for breakfast, you both can take your time getting ready." I gave them some space because it seemed like they didn't quite understand my need for personal space!

During breakfast, I called my family. Peter came to the breakfast area after some time, and I went to the room while Annie was still getting ready.

I told Annie that since I was using the single bed, she could sleep on one side of the double bed, opposite to me, and her husband on the other side. Annie said, "We are modern people, and there are no emotions attached to a hug. "If it were her daughter, she'd sleep on the single bed while she (Annie) faced her." My request to Annie was only to sleep on the opposite side of the double bed facing me. But her comment about being modern and there being no emotions attached to a hug clearly indicated that she was aware of how her husband has a tendency to touch or hug people, and, being a woman, she ignored it.

We gathered at the reception after breakfast. I asked the receptionist about the distances to the attractions I wanted to visit and also inquired if she had any local recommendations, as locals often have great insights for tourists. She marked the attractions on a map for me.

In contrast, Peter didn't believe in asking people for directions. He preferred to visit the places he liked and expected us to follow suit.

Tip: When you arrive at the hotel, ask the front desk staff to provide the name, address, and phone number in their native language. Also, remember to collect their business card.

Peter's usual habit was to put the attractions into Google Maps without checking the preferences of the others. Still, I told Annie and Peter that the receptionist marked attractions reachable by metro. Thinking Peter might keep asking for the map and bother me, I asked for another one from the receptionist with the same markings, so Annie and Peter had their own.

I accidentally left my phone at the reception, but thankfully, the receptionist gave it back before we took a taxi to the metro station. I was delighted with her gesture since my mobile was my only source for taking pictures, and I greatly enjoyed capturing photos of the places I visited.

Tip: It's advisable to provide a review for the staff member who assisted you during your night stay.

The taxi fare from our hotel in the industrial area to the nearest underground station, Rebbina, cost us 27 euros. While in the cab, Peter said that though the hotel was far, but he liked it. I replied, "It's Annie's choice." Firstly, I don't believe in taking credit for someone else's decision, and secondly, if he considered it far, then he should discuss it with his wife, who made the choice. After all, it's hard to find a hotel with everything – quality, affordability, and a central location. So, for a good price, it might be a bit farther from the city centre.

At the underground station, there was a machine to buy train tickets.

1. If you put in cash or coins, one journey costs 1.5 euros and is good for a single ride within the first 100 minutes after swiping your metro card.

2. If you use a credit card, one journey is 2 euros and stays valid for a single ride within the first 100 minutes after swiping your metro card.

Unfortunately, the vending machine wasn't accepting the credit card. Peter tends to be impatient and often insists on trying first, whether it's vending machines, McDonald's machines, or buying train tickets. I moved to another machine. I used coins, got my ticket, and a bit later, Peter said his card wasn't accepted. I pointed out that there was a technical fault indicated above the card slot. I then helped them with the purchase of tickets by using loose coins I had.

When we got to the stop for our first attraction, the receptionist had marked on the map a large park by the metro exit. We found the park nearby. It was quite sunny and I noticed that they were struggling to walk in the heat. After just 40 steps, they said, "Let's take pictures from here and leave."

I wondered what kind of sightseeing it was when we weren't actually exploring or enjoying the view of the attraction. I couldn't help but think that if the heat was making them uncomfortable, perhaps they shouldn't have left the hotel! I told Annie the way to a specific place, but in two minutes, he changed direction to skip that location and insisted we go straight to the Colosseum without taking our consent or checking if we wanted to skip that location. The Colosseum was indeed very crowded, and the hot weather didn't make it any more comfortable. As travellers, everyone's comfort and opinions are important, and it's insensitive to proceed without considering the interest of fellow travellers.

Tip: Before making any changes to the plans, ensure you have the consent of all travellers involved.

Annie and I stood in line to buy tickets for the attraction. While waiting, Peter called Annie and said there was someone from their community scalping tickets for 40 euros each, including a guide and a quick 40-minute tour. I was worried because Peter didn't seem interested in really seeing or enjoying the attraction; he wanted a fast 30-minute tour with a higher ticket cost. That's why I wasn't keen on going for that option.

If they wanted to go with that plan, I was fine with them spending 80 euros on themselves. After Annie hung up, I told her I'd talk to the security person in charge of the line to check the ticket price and estimated time when we'd get in. The security person said the ticket was 17 euros, and I thought I could get five coffees with the remaining 23 euros. I asked about the waiting time, and she explained they assign entry times like 2:30 PM, 2:45 PM, 3 PM, 3:15 PM, etc., once all the tickets are sold. Tourists must arrive at their designated time to enter the Colosseum. She also said the ticket booth was still open to buy tickets.

Tip: Travel buddies need to figure out whether they want to quickly see a place for a tick-box experience at double price or explore it leisurely without paying extra.

Tip: During travels, some opt for budget stays, while others prefer 5-star luxury. Some might save on attractions by observing from outside, while others value time and are willing to pay extra for convenience. Some wants to enjoy the experience in a leisurely manner. Since every traveller has a unique budget and preferences, it's crucial to journey with like-minded companions to prevent conflicts of choices.

I went back to where Annie was waiting and relayed the information. When our turn came at the ticket counter, the lady said they wouldn't issue a ticket to a third person if they weren't present there when buying, to prevent black market sales. Annie called Peter and instructed him to come to the counter immediately. When he arrived, I suggested that they should get their tickets at one counter, and I would buy mine at a different counter.

Our tickets indicated the entry time as 2:30 PM, but at the entrance, the guards said to come back at 2:15 PM because it was only 12:30 PM. The guard suggested we check out the adjacent attraction "Roman Forum and Palatine Hill," which was already included in our tickets. I thanked him for the info. I was completely okay with checking it out since it was covered by the ticket price, and we didn't have to spend our time waiting in line.

On the other hand, Peter shared his frustration with Annie, expressing they could have got a guided tour for just 40 euros. His frustrated face showed he was upset we didn't buy tickets on the black market.

I believe there are times when people don't have the same interests. Why insist on doing everything together? If they weren't comfortable, they could have proposed a specific time and place to meet later and we would have pursued our individual activities – they could have bought the tickets for 40 euros and quickly explored the Colosseum in 30 minutes while I'd have chosen a 17-euro ticket and taken my time exploring over 3 hours.

Peter wanted to go to the Palatine Hill. We were thirsty and they didn't have water bottles, so I gave one of mine to fill with tap water. We explored the extensive complex. Both Annie and I wore slippers instead of shoes that day, which was a bad choice as we had a hard time walking on uneven ground.

Tip: Before deciding on fancy footwear, check the streets around the attraction for even ground or uneven bricks; if they are uneven, opt for shoes instead.

While exploring, they saw a restaurant near the exit around 1 PM. I warned them that if they exited there, they couldn't come back to see the rest of the attractions. Once you swipe the ticket at the entrance, it only allows one entry, and trying to use it again means restricted access.

Annie suggested we split up, planning to meet near the Colosseum's entrance at 2:15 PM. I hurriedly explored everything, but I was glad to have seen it all. When I set a meeting time during an international trip, I always make sure to be on time. I got to the meeting spot at 2:15 PM. Eventually, we were allowed to enter at 2:30 PM. My friend Patricia had told me before the trip that there would be guided tours inside. She recommended joining one of those tours to learn about history without extra cost, as you just walk with the group and listen to the guide.

Tip: Stick close to a group with a guide; you will get to hear the history of the attraction for free!

Moreover, my primary focus wasn't on the historical aspect; I was more inclined towards capturing good photographs and experiencing the place visually.

I took pictures to share with my family who is really into history. When we left, it was already 4:15 PM. We saw a line at a small shop selling pizza slices. I suggested waiting if they wanted to, but they didn't, so we decided to find a restaurant together.

As we walked, Annie noticed I used to have lunch around 4-5 PM, my usual time even back home due to UK hours at work. It was 4:30 PM, and they were hungry, so we decided to grab a meal. While walking from the Colosseum to the restaurant, Annie said she was low on stamina and wanted to go back to the hotel after lunch. She said she won't be doing any more sightseeing. She further added that they didn't want to disrupt my plans or spoil my trip, encouraging me to go on without them. Post lunch, I agreed. I had the impression that their low stamina might be from not eating well.

We chose a nice restaurant called "Café de Art." They faced unexpected costs and financial setbacks because of the passport loss, like train fares, passport fees, photos, and even paying for the police report. So, I decided to treat them to a good, full meal since they'd been having smaller meals for the past 11 days.

We ordered a pizza, pasta, two cokes, and a pitcher of water. Even the water costs extra euros. I wanted Annie to enjoy a full meal instead of just half a burger. Annie wanted to chip in for the bill, but I insisted they consider it my birthday treat and accept it with gratitude.

After our meal at the restaurant, they felt more energized and were now excited to explore a few more attractions.

When they asked about our next stop, I told them there was an attraction near the Colosseum. Sadly, I couldn't get close enough for a photo because they started complaining about the weather. So, I took a photo from a distance and we went back to the metro station. I suggested trying to finish the trip with a single ticket, valid for 100 minutes, assuming it could cover both the way to our destination and back in that time.

While waiting for the train to the next attraction, the Spanish Steps, Annie expressed in a tone that conveyed slight agitation, that she would prioritize her health and if she didn't feel up to seeing the attraction, she would voice it. She further added that Peter hadn't slept well in last two days and seemed tired. She assured me that she had no issue with me going alone. I suggested returning to the hotel, willing to skip the attraction, recognizing that I was traveling with senior citizens. The tricky part was to explain that I didn't push for sightseeing after we checked-in - it was actually Peter who wanted to go out. He was taking charge of everything without consulting us and really wanted to explore the attractions because we had already missed a day in Rome and he didn't want to miss anything else.

We visited the Spanish Steps, surrounded by a high-end brand market. After checking out the area, we arrived at the metro station. On our way back, we bought tickets for a one-way journey within 100 minutes, planning to stick to our plan and return in that time. However, when we tried to use them for the return trip, they didn't work. So we had to buy new ones. Annie asked, "Did we go over the 100-minute limit?" The tickets were reasonably priced at 1.5 euros each, but Annie's comment left me feeling uneasy like there might be blame for maybe going over the time limit at one metro station. To sort it out, I responded, "I'll cover the metro expenses." By this time, Peter had purchased the tickets for all of us.

They appeared fatigued, especially Peter, and weren't up to seeing more attractions. Considering their fatigue, I compromised and suggested taking the current metro back to the hotel, planning to visit the attractions I missed on another trip to Rome and Milan in the future.

Out of the blue, Peter suggested getting off at the next metro stop to see the Trevi Fountain. Annie seemed unsure about it. But, when we neared the station, he insisted on getting off to see the attraction. I was deeply touched by his thoughtful gesture.

The Trevi Fountain is a must-see. After getting off the metro, it was a 10-minute walk, and I asked if they felt like walking for another 10 minutes. Peter suggested having a beer at one of the open-air restaurants, and I was fine with it. I didn't mind what they decided to eat or not eat. When you order for yourself, you usually choose without thinking much, but when you're with someone, you pay more attention to what to order, especially thinking about the costs.

While they enjoyed their beer, I quickly walked, almost ran, being careful with my knee. I have a slightly weak right knee due to a bad fall I had when I was a child. My doctor had advised me to be cautious and avoid any further stress on the knee. I reached the attraction and took several photos in just 3 minutes. But I couldn't fully enjoy the view, I wanted to sit and spend time savouring it. I was okay; at least, I caught a glimpse of the attraction, thanks to Peter's support.

I joined them after 25 minutes. Annie said they enjoyed ice cream and beer. I informed her I finished exploring, thanked her, and suggested going back to the hotel. At the metro station, Annie asked the security about our tickets, explaining we bought them 20 minutes ago, and that they should still be valid since we didn't go over the 100-minute limit. The security person clarified that the 100 minutes were only for leaving the station, and since we had one-way tickets, we couldn't use them again even if there was time left. Annie understood then, but her earlier comment already gave me an idea of what she was thinking.

After sightseeing, we reached the underground station. It was already 7:30 PM, and Peter's phone only had 4% battery left. Annie's phone had died, and I was surprised because she hadn't made calls or used the internet much to drain it. My phone's battery was down to 12% from taking lots of photos, and I didn't have much data left. Unfortunately, none of us had a power bank. If I had known, I wouldn't have left it in the hotel. I also tried Uber, but it didn't seem to work either.

Tip: Always carry a power bank.

Unfortunately, every taxi we tried to book was cancelling on us. While waiting at the taxi stand, a person of sketchy looks came to buy juice from the underground station. This situation was unsettling as it was getting dark, there was an unfamiliar presence, and Italy is known for safety concerns, especially with certain individuals, making it not the safest place. While Peter was busy booking Uber, Annie quietly commented to me, "We didn't return by 5 to the hotel."

On Day 1 of our travel, I told Annie that my friends back home suggested returning by 5-6 PM. But in all our trips before Rome, we always got back to the hotel after 8 PM. In Amsterdam, we once left the hotel as late as 9 PM and came back close to midnight. On this occasion, Annie remarked we weren't following the "return by 5" rule. I had the urge to ask if they were thinking of sticking to a 5-7 PM schedule now, as I was eager to explore the attractions.

Over the past six days, we consistently came back to the hotel at 8 PM after our daily sightseeing. It left me pondering why Annie hadn't mentioned earlier that this timing might not be safe. Interestingly, this lack of concern about timing was consistent even when they lost their passports in Amsterdam, a city also known for safety concerns. No sarcastic comments were made to Peter about being extra cautious. In my case, Annie commented, 'We didn't return by 5'. Even when we ventured out at 9 PM to explore the Red-Light district in Amsterdam and returned by midnight, which was the attraction they were eager to see, no remarks were made about the timing. If Annie was genuinely concerned about safety and intended to stick to the routine of returning between 5 to 6 PM, it raises the question of why she and Peter wanted to explore the Red-Light area after 9 PM. During that time, the concept of sticking to the usual 5 to 6 PM timings didn't seem to be a priority for Annie, as she didn't appear apprehensive.

In Amsterdam, the situation was quite unique. I could also have jokingly said something about the relaxed attitude causing the passport loss, which affected my future travel plans. However, I decided not to use sarcasm. I was there to help them during tough times. In this recent situation, it wasn't a loss; it was just about not finding a taxi. During the passport loss incident, I mentioned that "we are all in this together", and now, she was pointing out that you had planned to return to the hotel by 5-6 PM.

Annie's comment made me lose the respect I had for them, even though they were supportive despite their low stamina. In the past few days, we didn't stick to any timing rules. On this day we couldn't find a taxi or Uber and she decided to make a sarcastic comment. Returning from Amsterdam at 11:30 PM, especially given the circumstances of the Red-Light area, was indeed unusual. If we had missed the last train back to the hotel, I too should have made a sarcastic remark, but that's not how I handle things.

Not getting a cab made Peter comment that the hotel should have been booked in the main part right in the middle of the city.

I promptly replied that Annie chose the hotel because it was cost-effective. It was my indirect way of telling Peter that whether the hotel choice was good or bad, they should take responsibility, whether for credit or blame, and keep me out of it.

All of a sudden, I spotted a representative wearing a tie, which seemed to be a dress code. I mentioned to Annie that I would speak to her for assistance. I introduced myself from the aviation industry and noting her scarf, which indicated a possible customer service background, I explained our predicament. I mentioned we were stuck due to taxi cancelations and asked for her assistance. The lady was incredibly kind and supportive. She lived near the underground station and even telephoned her husband to join us.

Peter suddenly interrupted, perhaps attempting to take credit (during the embassy incident when I informed people about the lost passports, and he snapped at me to let him speak). This time, the situation was reversed, and I had a choice: should I respond sharply or withdraw from the conversation, I chose the latter. Having one person speak is often more effective than approaching someone with three individuals seeking help which can appear quite intimidating.

When dealing with strangers, it's important to remember that we are strangers to them too. In this case, it was 8 PM and as a woman, it's reasonable to assume she likely had her own safety concerns.

Conversation between two women usually feels more comfortable, and Peter's involvement might have been seen as an interruption. It can be unsettling when someone unfamiliar jumps into a conversation. Regrettably, some people lack the proper etiquette and tend to intervene. At that moment, I thought, "Let him take the credit if he wants to." I stepped away, feeling annoyed by his behaviour to solely claim credit for getting us out of that situation.

In Amsterdam, when Andrew went to meet the counsellor, Peter wanted us to share the long story with him. I quietly told Annie that I'd handle the conversation to avoid sending mixed messages to Andrew. I requested Annie to explain to her husband that I intended to manage the situation in my own manner because these contacts were known to me. Annie explained it to Peter in their language, saying I would handle the conversation, and he shouldn't interfere. When Andrew returned, Peter attempted to join the conversation. I politely (didn't snap like he did to me at the Berne embassy) asked him to wait and made it clear I wanted to proceed in my own way, focusing on relevant information.

As the lady arranged the cab, Peter suggested I convey to the lady that if we couldn't find a taxi, we could go to her house briefly. I wasn't comfortable with saying this to her, and I suggested Peter convey it directly. However, Peter insisted that I tell her, expressing that it wouldn't be appropriate for him to do so and that we wouldn't enter her house but wait outside for safety. Yet, when I conveyed this, she didn't respond. It's worth contemplating what you would do in a situation like this. I found it strange because he usually jumps into the conversation. He could have asked his wife to convey the message, but instead, he asked me to do it.

In my view, self-inviting, even if it's just to wait outside, may not be well-received by strangers, particularly when abroad. It has the potential to make the person offering assistance uncomfortable, leading them to disengage. However, in this case, she didn't voice objections; instead, she smiled and chose to disregard the request. Nevertheless, she ensured the taxi arrived as planned.

Her husband arrived, and she introduced him to us. He had arranged a taxi, but the driver had trouble finding us. The driver initially entered the middle lane and missed us. He made a U-turn and reached the third lane whereas we were waiting in the first lane all this while. Her husband was helpful and guided the driver to the first lane to ensure the taxi arrived. We showed the business card of the hotel to the driver. We were relieved to board the taxi and thanked the couple for their assistance and I conveyed, "May God fulfil all your wishes and desires in life, sending you many blessings." Interestingly, this taxi driver charged us 13 euros, compared to the morning taxi which cost 27 euros. As a token of appreciation, we rounded off the fare to 15 euros.

Tip: When you arrive at a hotel in an unfamiliar area, be sure to collect the hotel's business cards. This makes it easy to show the address to taxi drivers.

Indeed, Annie made a comment of return by 5 PM rule, but it's crucial to remember it was an unusual situation that could happen to anyone. Moreover, my proactive efforts played a key role in resolving the situation. Taking the initiative and showing some presence of mind, I approached the lady wearing the scarf, recognizing her potential connection to the aviation industry or a related field. The way I communicated and the references I used had a significant impact. The key point is – it's not just about asking for help; it's about how you communicate and engage in conversation with the other person. My approach made a significant difference, and she arranged a taxi for us.

The respect for the entire day, considering their participation in sightseeing despite low stamina, washed out because of her one sarcastic comment.

Peter settled the taxi fare at the hotel, and I recorded it in the expense diary.

I wanted to give them some time to rest and settle comfortably in the room, so I used the restroom in the lobby. While in the lobby, I decided to have dinner.

I thoughtfully called them from the reception to their hotel room, asking if they'd like to join me for dinner at the hotel restaurant. Consistent with their cost-conscious tendencies, they declined.

I ordered pasta in green sauce and a coffee, and although the pasta had an unexpected taste resembling non-vegetarian dishes, I enjoyed my meal. Upon returning to the room, I found them savouring their homemade theplas with curd. Annie offered some to me, but as I'm not a fan of Indian food, I politely declined. Peter then inquired about my meal, I mentioned having pasta and coffee. Annie shared that Peter had slight fever, so she gave him some medicine.

The next day, I asked Peter how he was feeling, and he confirmed that he was doing fine in his usual energetic voice. As we were getting ready to go to Florence, I finished the check-out at the hotel. I told Annie and Peter that I'd meet them in the hotel's reception area. After checking out, I left my luggage with the reception staff and grabbed a couple of croissants for a mid-morning snack. They didn't realize that Peter had left his jacket in their room when they checked out.

We got into the taxi, and I told Annie that I would pay for the taxi this time since Peter had already covered the expenses for the two previous taxis. I prefer to balance out expenses during travels in different countries to keep things fair among travel companions. Annie agreed, but Peter started talking to Annie in his language which I didn't understand. His expression suggested he was not pleased with me covering the fare. I could sense that there was some underlying financial concern, though I only fully understood his intention to collect money from me towards the end of the trip. I restated to Annie that I aim for fair expense-sharing, explaining why I volunteered to cover the taxi cost.

Peter's undisclosed intentions made me uneasy, it seemed there was something he wasn't sharing, ultimately contributing to a dampened mood.

While stories about theft or safety concerns in Italy might circulate, my personal experience was remarkably positive with locals. They went above and beyond to assist us, helping us secure transportation and even returning a lost mobile phone.

Traveling and exploring teach you geography and history, while adventures offer valuable life lessons.

Chapter 6

Questionable Sightseeing: Rushing Through Florence

We reached Termini station in Rome in order to catch our train to Florence. I suggested standing in a corner for safety, so we only had to watch the front, left, and right. With a wall behind, we could protect one side instead of being open to people from all sides.

The display didn't show the platform yet because it usually appears 30 minutes before the train leaves. Despite a scary incident in Amsterdam, we stuck to our routine and arrived early again. We waited for the platform number as our train was delayed. Peter suggested I watch our three bags while he and Annie looked for the platform. I said no, as it wouldn't be safe for one person to handle all the luggage in a crowded place where anyone could come from any side.

Annie went alone to find the platform but couldn't get any info. To ease his worry, I suggested checking a nearby shop, though I knew the screen usually had details. I inquired with the sales representative about why the platform information wasn't visible and if she had any suggestions. She explained that the incoming train was delayed, causing a change in the scheduled time from 8:15 AM to 8:45 AM. She mentioned that the platform for the outbound train wouldn't be assigned until the delayed incoming train received its platform assignment. She also made it clear that we had no choice but to wait for the display board to update. The logical approach dictated that if the board was displaying information, we should rely on it. I relayed the information. Peter's frustration grew, and he kept looking for info elsewhere even though the display board clearly showed 'DELAYED'. He even went to check at the information desk, but the board updated the platform details while he was away.

Just like at the airport where they assign the gate only when the estimated time of arrival (ETA) is known, the display board gets updated with the gate number. In today's world, everything has transitioned to self-sufficiency with electronic updates, reducing the need for face-to-face interactions.

When you travel abroad, people often advise you to check signboards for info instead of asking others. So, it puzzled me when someone, whom I considered an intellectual, suggested going to the inquiry counter. The train wasn't cancelled but merely delayed. Typically, face-to-face interactions with an executive are necessary when dealing with a cancelation, and it seemed they didn't fully grasp the difference between these terms. We eventually boarded the train once the platform was assigned.

When we arrived at the Florence train station, I observed that Peter, who usually rushes on and off trains without looking for escalators or elevators, faced a staircase of about 10-15 steps with our bags. I pointed out a slanted path for rolling luggage, but Peter chose the stairs, thinking the other way would take longer. While my bag was light, I was surprised he didn't consider the effort for both him and his wife with two big bags. In my opinion, it's much more convenient to roll a suitcase than to carry a large bag up or down the stairs. I offered to help with their suitcases many times, but Peter said no. So, we carried our own luggage down the stairs.

We had booked an Airbnb in Florence. I trailed behind them to the Airbnb. In Europe, roads are often crafted with diverse brick materials, especially in historic city centers and older towns, lending them a charming and traditional ambiance. The uneven and rough nature of these roads can indeed lead to wheel and tire damage, which is precisely what occurred in my case. Peter expressed the idea that I should consider purchasing a new bag.

I prefer smart suggestions over obvious solutions. So, when it comes to travel, I tend to rely on my own thinking more than external suggestions. My bag was relatively new, only used it twice. Handling two suitcases can be tougher (one duffle bag and one medium-sized bag). With the front wheels damaged, I flipped my bags, using the back wheels for easier dragging. We reached our Airbnb by walking with the help of Google Maps.

Before our trip, I mentioned a downside of this Airbnb – the neighbourhood had reviews of sketchy people hanging around, drinking, and smoking making it feel a bit intimidating. When we got there, we saw the place had one bedroom with a bathroom, a kitchen with a washing machine, and a double bed in the living room. I took the living room spot, and they picked the double bed. I was happy we had a washing machine. Annie said she'd wash her clothes first, and then I could do mine.

Whenever they asked about sightseeing ideas, I always gave a neutral response, like "We can go there, I'm neutral". I did this because I knew Peter would go with his own preferences and might blame me if things went awry. I'm glad I didn't suggest much; it saved me from many accusations. I let them choose freely without getting upset if they didn't pick the attractions I suggested. Instead, my critique was how they experience the attractions, they should take more time enjoying the attractions, not just rush through them in 3 minutes.

It's really odd to quickly see the lovely views in Florence in just three minutes and then rush to catch a bus. Looking back, Peter should have mentioned if he likes visiting sights quickly before we left the Airbnb. Then, I could have made a different plan, like staying in my room and doing laundry.

They weren't really into sightseeing on their Europe trip; instead, they wanted to show their relatives at a family gathering that they visited many places in Europe. For them, it was a brief excursion.

Tip: If you're only planning to spend 3 minutes at a place, maybe skip international travel and enjoy the scenic beauty in magazines instead.

In the morning, I suggested that we visit Michelangelo's Point, a spot offering a panoramic view of the entire city. But Peter insisted on visiting the David Statue instead. They really wanted to see the Michelangelo David statue, so we went to the museum. At the ticket counter, Peter insisted on buying tickets for all three of us. Normally, I prefer getting my own ticket to avoid the stress of detailed expense records and figuring out who owes what, but I agreed without objecting. Towards the end of the trip, I understood why he insisted.

Adjacent to the ticket counter, there was a shop catering to gym-goers with light groceries and snacks available.

Peter asked if I was interested in a Coke or ice cream, but I declined and told them they were welcome to order whatever they liked. They decided to get a Coke and split it between them, and if I had joined in, it would have been dividing it into thirds, which isn't really my preference.

In a group, sharing food and drinks can be great if everyone likes the same things. But if tastes are different, be aware that paying individually is better. Otherwise, you might end up paying much more for something small, like a burger, when sharing. Abroad, one is paying 6 times the price compared to Indian money.

Tip: Travel buddies should buy their own meals at the counter (McDonalds, Starbucks, etc.). This way, everyone pays for their own food, which avoids any surprises, especially if some items like meat dishes or drinks are pricey.

After that, we stood in a line, and they met people from their community. So they started chatting in their language, leaving me out. So, I decided to move forward in the line, letting them talk without feeling like they had to include me. Even if I stayed, it wouldn't have mattered because I didn't understand their language. Standing there not understanding their conversation seemed pointless. That was the second time I noticed Peter being remarkably polite to strangers.

I found solace in my own company. At the security checkpoint, we had to put our bags through a scanner, and they told me to throw away my bottle. I was upset they made me do that. Typically, I carry a big bottle and a small one, refilling the small one from the big one. I also share water with friends who run out. I think museums have this rule to protect valuable paintings from spills. So, it's better not to bring large bottles to museums, as they might make you throw them away.

Tip: Don't take bottles to museums because they might make you throw them away. Museum security is pretty strict about this, and they won't let you keep the empty bottle, even if you try to empty it.

I'm not really into history, and when we went into the Michelangelo David Museum where there is a display of a 17-foot-tall naked statue of David, there's only so much you can admire or read. So, to give Peter a taste of leaving early, I tried his trick by saying, "Let's go in 5 minutes; I'm done with the museum." But this time, he wanted to stay longer and enjoy more time. Surprisingly, Annie revealed that her son doesn't like traveling with the family because Peter rushes through things. Her son would prefer to take more time, which Peter might not like.

In Rome, I saw he usually wanted to leave attractions after only 3-4 minutes. But this time, he wanted to stay longer because he wanted to fully enjoy the statue of David. It surprised me that they spent a good 45 minutes to an hour there without rushing. Maybe they decided to stay longer at the Michelangelo David Museum because they bought tickets and wanted to get the full experience. For attractions where they didn't buy tickets, they preferred leaving in 3-4 minutes.

A few days ago in Amsterdam, we spent a few hours exploring the Red-Light district and today we spent another hour at the Michelangelo David statue. But for iconic European beauties like the Trevi Fountain and the Spanish Steps, which are famous worldwide for their beauty, he'd only spend 3 minutes. I could never understand why his approach was different. It made me wonder what he found more beautiful: the Michelangelo David statue, the Red-Light district, or these other European marvels. Maybe the statue or the Red-Light district had a special appeal for him.

After the Michelangelo David Museum, Peter suggested, "Let's go to Michelangelo's Point," and he checked Google Maps for directions. Annie and I just went along, as we had shortlisted this attraction while preparing our list of attractions to see in the morning, and I was neutral, willing to go wherever they decided to visit.

I was delighted that he picked the same place Annie and I wanted to visit in Florence. Using Google Maps, Peter tried to find the way to Michelangelo's viewpoint for a panoramic view of Florence, but he had trouble finding one. We eagerly followed him, only to be led astray, costing us an hour and a half.

Since we were together, I thought I'd try and ask a shopkeeper for directions. But the route seemed far and necessitated taking a bus. Peter disagreed, insisting it was close, even though he had already led us to the wrong places before. His excessive confidence wasted a lot of our time.

The shopkeeper's advice and the acknowledgment of a longer distance turned out to be right when we decided to take the bus for a scenic view in Florence the next day.

Tip: If you're ever unsure of your way in a city or lost, consider asking someone who's out walking their dog or a shopkeeper for directions; chances are, they're quite familiar with the area.

Unfortunately, Peter never considered asking for directions. As a traveller, it's essential to set aside time to find the address, sort out transportation, and handle everything else related to the location.

Tip: Spend 10 minutes planning your route and activities before you start; it helps avoid wandering without a purpose.

Anyway, when we couldn't find the place, we decided to take a casual walk in the market without a specific plan. Then Peter mentioned they wanted ice cream. I was already having some trouble with my wisdom tooth, so I hesitated. Annie kindly gave me some medicine, and I was really thankful for that. At 6:35 PM, we found a gelato ice cream parlor where one cup cost 6.5 euros. Peter bought a cup with three spoons, suggesting we share it to help with my toothache. I was surprised by the idea of sharing ice cream with a married couple and had concerns. Even if we use our own spoons, dipping them into the same cup of ice cream which might have saliva seemed unhygienic. Plus, I was dealing with a mouth infection and didn't want to risk spreading it. I excused myself to explore the shop, thinking it was better to give space to people eating, and ordered my own ice cream cone to enjoy separately. I didn't share as I like having a whole meal to myself. In your own country, it's more common to share because you're using your own money. But when you're spending 100 bucks for a snack in your home country, that same snack could cost you six times more, like 600 bucks, in another country. That's why you are less inclined to share in those situations.

Also, travellers prefer to order their individual meals. Plus, when meeting friends over a cup of coffee in your country, it's common to share snacks by dividing them equally because it's not a full meal. This is acceptable, as you typically plan to have lunch and dinner at home. However, during foreign trips, you often skip snacks and focus on having hearty lunches and dinners, or sometimes just one good full meal, to ensure you have the energy for sightseeing.

Also, unless you're traveling with your parents or your immediate family, sharing meals is typical. However, when you're with friends, it's common practice for each person to cover their own meal expenses.

After enjoying a gelato, we ventured into a shop that featured crochet tops. I ran out of water in my water bottle, and my hands were a bit sticky from the ice cream. Adjacent to the shop, there was a restaurant nearby. But, I thought if I went there with three people and asked for water, they might say no because some places charge for water and using the restroom. Even if I asked for water for two more bottles, there was a chance of being refused. While they were busy looking at the dresses, I quickly went to the restaurant. Smartly, I told the bartender I had a sore throat and asked for tap water. Since my bottle was only around 200 ml, he kindly gave me some tap water. I used it to wet a tissue, clean my hands, and soothe my throat. When I got back to the crochet shop, I told them I got tap water and suggested they could ask the bartender if they wanted some too.

Tip: Carry a small 200ml bottle with you and ask any restaurant to fill it citing a health condition like sore throat. In Europe, water is typically charged for, but if you request to refill a 200ml bottle due to a throat infection, you might receive water for free.

My guess was right because the bartender said no when both Annie and Peter went together, each with their large-sized bottles.

By 7:30 PM, we came across a market with premium brands. Suddenly, Peter got worried about having less money, left with around 40 euros, and wondered if the 100 euros were misused or if the morning cab driver overcharged him on his card. I reminded him that I used my credit card to pay for the cab in the morning, not him. I also mentioned considering the museum fee, and after calculating, he felt relieved that the remaining balance was satisfactory. We reached our Airbnb apartment by 7:50 PM. There were two people hefty guys nearby, enjoying drinks and cigarettes. Right across from our apartment, there was a single store that offered groceries, alcohol, and everyday items like toothpaste and toothbrushes. Peter wanted to buy some beer for himself.

I noticed Peter started taking out a lot of money from his pocket, with many 10 or 20-euro notes outside the apartment. I couldn't help but think that displaying money like that on the street could cause unnecessary problems. It's important to keep track of how much you have in each pocket and only take out what you need, instead of pulling out many 20-euro notes.

Tip: Avoid flashy displays of wealth. Keep valuable items out of sight, refrain from showing money in public and avoid displaying expensive jewellery or gadgets.

Peter's handling of the cash was noticeable, even from a distance. Muggers typically focus on someone with money in hand, not the amount. I expressed my worry to Annie about her husband's safety, especially since the two hefty guys who were sitting outside had also headed to the same shop after Peter went in. I suggested we go to the shop to be with Peter, ensuring his safety and offering support.

She concurred, and when we entered the shop, we found it quite small. The shopkeeper recommended that we, the ladies, come inside because the two men outside were troublesome, and he would follow us. Therefore, we stood behind the counter as instructed. The shopkeeper told the two men that we were his sisters and visiting him, urging them not to cause any harm.

It was quite kind of him. Then, Peter took out a couple of 20 euro notes again. I remarked, "What are you doing? You're drawing attention," and Annie scolded her husband too. I noticed this repeated behaviour both in the Brussels underground station and this shop in Rome. Both his wife and I often warned him not to continue with this behaviour because it could lead to problems for him.

While this was happening, a tall man entered the shop and began observing us, which felt uneasy. In my view, one should simply buy what was needed and go back to the apartment right across the street. Peter was excited about the 2-euro beer, which he found reasonably priced. I thought, "Is he so focused on beer that he's not thinking about paying and going back to the apartment?" Annie asked if I wanted anything, and I said, "None." I didn't plan to drink. Eventually, she bought two cans of Coke.

Back in our apartment, Annie cooked some Maggi and soup, and I handled the dishes. Peter enjoyed his beer, and they shared a can of Coke. I couldn't help but chuckle when

Peter started giving me advice on how much soap to use when cleaning the pans. In a light-hearted manner, I joked with him that he shouldn't get involved in household chores. Then, I suggested the idea of visiting Pisa the next day, and they agreed.

The next day, we went to Pisa, which was a 40-minute train ride away. At the train station, I recommended waiting in line to buy our tickets. After I got mine, I called them over so they wouldn't have to wait for the next representative and could purchase their tickets. Towards the end of the trip, I realized they expected me to buy their tickets too. It would have been easier if everyone covered their own expenses, avoiding the need to keep track of shared costs.

Upon reaching Pisa station, we took a bus. During the journey, he mentioned not wanting to go to the entrance or climb the Pisa Tower. I speculated it might be due to cost or age restrictions. Considering his thrifty nature and habitual checking of route and entrance fees (around 30 euros per person) to the Pisa Tower, it seemed he was saving 60 euros for Annie and himself by not purchasing tickets.

It was clear that Peter wasn't keen on enjoying the view from the top of the Pisa Tower. This became obvious as I never saw him buy tickets for any attractions, except for four specific ones that caught his interest: the Heineken Museum in Amsterdam, Adam's Lookout in Amsterdam, the Colosseum in Rome, and Michelangelo's statue of David in Florence.

It started appearing that Peter had no interest in getting tickets or staying there for an extended time. Going to an attraction is a tick-box exercise for him to show to others that he travelled there. His plan was to return quickly or perhaps even earlier, and I had no objections to that. I believed that we were visiting the attractions at the very least, so I chose to remain silent.

Photos

I wasn't happy with how they were taking pictures with the background often turning out to be blurry. So, I started asking others to take my photos. They went into the crowd, and I hurried to find them. I asked them again to take pictures at a couple of spots, but the photos weren't great. Nonetheless, I was able to capture some good shots of them.

I asked them a few times to take pictures, but they didn't do a good job. It seemed like they weren't interested in capturing my photos, as their photography seemed more like a formality, and taking photos was more of a routine for them. I thought it might be best not to bother them for pictures in case they had other things to do or wanted to go fast.

I didn't mind; if that's how they wanted things to be, I'll just ask someone else for photos. Negative feelings would likely manifest in the pictures or the way they're taken. If it's not on purpose to spoil my photos, it seemed like they had minimal interest in photographing me and were more focused on exploring and leaving the location quickly.

While in Pisa, I captured a picture of them so beautifully that it could have been a perfect addition to their home decor.

But when Annie tried to take a photo, she had trouble getting the angle right and seemed a bit uninterested, so some random people in the background ended up in the shot. It's a bummer when people lack the sensitivity to capture a memorable picture, especially when we had limited time in Pisa, just 15-20 minutes according to her husband's plan.

We stayed in Pisa only for 20 minutes before leaving, and I noticed that Peter preferred spending more time traveling in buses and trains rather than fully appreciating the beauty of the destinations people travel to see. On the train back from Pisa, Annie made a valid observation that the first day is usually spent figuring out the place, like elevators and exits. By the second day, we're better at it, but then we have to start getting ready for the next destination. The first day is always a bit tricky.

When we got to Florence station, they decided to make up for the fancy meal in Rome by treating me to gelato ice cream.

At the train station, we saw a large underground complex similar to Janpath, offering a wide range of items from groceries and clothing to shoes and electronics. Annie and I wanted to check out one of the shops, and Peter, in his language, said to Annie, "Saturday market," indicating that we were entering every shop.

Peter wanted to find out the cost of the multi-plug adapter since they'd been using mine for the last four days. I estimated it to be at least 10 euros. Upon his return, Peter said it was exactly 10 euros. I proposed that they continue using my adapter and cord to avoid additional expenses for the remaining ten days, and they agreed.

After a few minutes, we found a good brand and bought some clothes. While I was waiting to pay at the cashier's counter, I remembered my experience of shopping in Antwerp and inquired about the VAT refund. The shopkeeper informed me that the minimum purchase had to exceed 150 euros.

I then explained the VAT refund process to Annie and suggested combining our purchases to claim the refund at the airport. Annie agreed, and while she and Peter waited, the shopkeeper took his time with the paperwork. Given the hot weather, I asked for water. In Europe, it's not always free, and the shopkeeper got only half a glass, which I handed to Annie. The shopkeeper gave me a paper fan when he saw that I was hot, and I handed it to Annie so she could cool down as well. After leaving, Annie saw a grocery store nearby, but Peter advised against buying anything.

Food

After our quick shopping, Annie asked if I had a sandwich, but I had already eaten mine. I was taken aback by the recurring pattern of Annie asking me for food or soft drinks. For instance, during our time in Amsterdam, she noticed that I had purchased a Starbucks sandwich in the morning, and by noon, she asked if I could give it to her and her husband. On another day in Amsterdam, she asked for a Coca-Cola that I had purchased the day before. Similarly, in Florence, she inquired if I had a sandwich to share. It's funny because she often asks for meals from me, especially outside stores or restaurants, without buying anything for herself.

Upon learning that I didn't have any sandwiches in my bag, she explained that they eat less in the morning and tend to get hungry around 1 or 2 PM and need something to eat. I said if they were hungry, they should have told me earlier, and we could have stopped for a meal. I thought, 'Who's stopping them from buying food for themselves?' Anyhow, Annie said they would prepare something at the apartment. She continued to remark that I have my lunch at 4 PM, which aligns with my customary eating time in my home country. I agreed with her observation. She continued by saying that I usually don't feel hungry before 4 PM because I often have a sandwich as a snack in the meantime. Again, I acknowledged. She said that they needed lunch and wanted to go to the apartment to make it.

As we were heading back to the apartment, I remembered that in the morning, they had bhujiya and tea for breakfast and had also set aside a coffee for me. I explained that I don't eat bhujiya and prefer my sandwich, so I would enjoy that instead. I asked if they had eaten breakfast, and she mentioned that they had already eaten namkeen. I responded I usually don't have those for breakfast and preferred a sandwich. Since I had my meal after their breakfast, it didn't make sense for them to ask for a portion of my sandwich. I thoroughly relished my tomato sauce sandwich; it was absolutely delicious!

When we reached the apartment entrance, Peter decided to buy beer from the same grocery store outside our apartment. Annie asked what I wanted. With a sore throat, I suggested juice and let them decide. I didn't plan to buy anything and had no coins. Back in the apartment, I put my water mug in the freezer to cool it up for my parched throat. Annie suggested doing the same for the juice. After 10 minutes, I drank my water and felt relieved. I had also put my small water bottle in the fridge on the side and not in the freezer. After eating, I took my water, but the juice was still in the fridge. This happened before we left for Michelangelo's Point.

Annie and I planned to split a Coke, and Peter, enjoying his beer, couldn't resist taking some of the Coke from Annie. He asked her to share, I didn't get how someone could enjoy the taste of Coke while drinking beer. Peter surprised me with his behaviour towards his wife, not even letting her enjoy half a glass of Coke.

Peter could've enjoyed his beer, letting his wife fully enjoy her half of the Coke. When she shared it with him, it became just another half. It would've been nice if he allowed her to enjoy her drink without any interruption. Peter should've thought more about his wife's enjoyment.

Annie cooked lunch, and we ate together. Since my tooth was hurting, making me a bit grumpy, I chose to concentrate on packing.

Before we left for Pisa in the morning, Annie had already loaded the dirty clothes into the washing machine. After lunch, she took them out and hung them to dry. Surprisingly, she didn't say I could use the machine for my laundry. When I suggested it, Peter quickly said no because we were leaving in the morning. I felt both Annie and Peter were being a bit selfish.

On our first day in Florence, Annie said she'd wash her clothes first, and I could wash after her. But she used the machine on the second day instead of the first. This left me limited time to wash and dry my clothes since we had to leave the apartment early on the third day. Peter strongly opposed my use of the machine by stating, "Don't use the machine, we are leaving early tomorrow morning."

After lunch, Peter took a nap, so Annie and I began packing because we were going to Venice the next day. They didn't decide to go to Michelangelo's Point until 4 PM.

We left the apartment at 4:15 PM and waited at the bus stop for 20 minutes, but the bus didn't show up. While waiting, I told Peter to remember the bus stop's name, but he was busy with his phone, so he asked me to write it down. Then, I suggested to Annie to take a picture of the bus stop's name for our way back. Annie commented that she wouldn't take out her phone. I usually don't take my phone out in busy places to avoid it being snatched, and I save battery for photos. At that moment, there wasn't any crowd at the bus stop, and I didn't want to take out my phone out of laziness. Annie's comment stung a bit, but I realized she might think I wasn't using my phone at all. I don't use my phone for Google Maps to save data, and I enjoy finding my own way, unlike Peter who relies heavily on Google Maps.

Tip: Using GPS is great, but it's also important to trust your own sense of direction. Knowing your way around without relying on technology is useful in case your phone runs out of battery.

It's upsetting because Annie forgot I used my international number to call the hotels before the trip to figure out distances and commuting info. Even during the trip, I used my phone to call hotels for the best routes. Annie's comment only focused on me not taking a picture of the bus stop. They didn't recognize my phone use for gathering location and travel info, and that's a bit hurtful.

We got to Michelangelo's Point at 5:30 PM because we left late from the apartment, and the place was a bit far.

The view was breathtaking. After 3-8 minutes of our arrival, Peter informed us our return bus had arrived, and the next one would be at 9 PM, so we had to board that one.

They began walking towards the bus, and I told them I would catch up. I found a friendly lady from my country and asked her to take photos of me, and she did a great job. She took pictures from various angles, making a special memory with beautiful photos. I quickly caught up with Annie and Peter and we boarded the bus.

Peter's insistence to leave the Florence view in 8 minutes didn't leave a positive impression. I didn't suggest a nap in the afternoon. We paid 6 euros to get there, but for what reason, to see Florence for 8 minutes.

As travellers, we often spend a lot of money, sometimes hundreds of thousands. It's not good when someone keeps interrupting our plans or makes decisions that cut short the trip/sightseeing. It can really spoil the travel experience for everyone.

We reached our apartment. Peter went to his room, and for the first time, Annie spent some time with me, engaging in a light conversation.

Suddenly, Annie got a call and went to the open kitchen to talk in her own language. A few minutes later, my best friend called me. But it was noisy in the background, and my voice was strained from a sore throat. My friend suggested I go outside for a clearer conversation.

When I came back, Annie was still on her call. Then, I got another call and told Annie her voice was loud, so I stepped outside the apartment to continue the call. Later, Peter came out and told me that they had finished their call, and I could come back inside to talk. Since I couldn't understand their language or the context of their conversation, there was no reason for me to allow them to listen to my phone call conversation with my friends. My need for personal space was important to me. When I got back, they had already eaten, so I made soup for myself because of my toothache.

That night, I tallied up the day's expenses, counting even small amounts like 1 or 2 euros. I also packed my things and shared the daily expenses report in the group, listing transactions from 1 euro to 30 euros before going to sleep.

Tip: When you travel with others, it's good to use a shared application to track everyone's daily expenses.

In the morning, Peter and Annie began speaking in their language. Peter's loud voice showed he wasn't happy about something. I could tell he was talking about the expense details I shared with them because he used the words "euro to euro" in English while talking to Annie. I concentrated on sorting my things as they didn't include me in the conversation. Otherwise, they would have spoken in a language I could understand.

Out of nowhere, Peter said to me, "Yeh kya 1 euro ka hisaab hain. (Why bother with these small amounts? What's the fuss about 1 euro?)." I clarified I'm giving the details of the expenses incurred. And, 1 euro is like 100 times our currency, so neglecting even 1 euro spent daily for a month on them would mean losing 60 euros, which is 6,000 rupees in our currency. And the amount doubles up to 12000 rupees for spending 1 euro on two people. I must admit, his idea was clever. Then he spoke in his language, and I caught a few words like 'euro ka euro main.' I thought he might be saying that euro transactions should be in euros, just like I mentioned at the beginning of the trip.

He insisted on adding up all expenses and split them equally among the three of us. But, if I spent 100 euros, why should I share it equally with three people? Doing that could either make me lose money or gain a profit, depending on different situations.

The main thing is, why should I take someone else's money or pay more than my fair part? If I spent 10,000, I should be able to explain each expense, saying where and how much was spent, and that's what I expect from them too.

Naturally, he'd be keeping track of transactions given his thrifty nature. However, I sensed that something else was bothering him. When he questioned why I was noting down 1 euro expenses, I explained that having a record of everyone's spending helps avoid confusion and provides clarity. If I only give a total without the daily details, you might ask about the big amount, needing more explanations. It's more practical to record expenses daily. Still, he insisted, saying, "Just tell me the total and my share, that's all."

When Peter suggested splitting expenses by three, I realized he might be trying to take advantage. I was okay with giving the total amount, but I wanted everyone to have a clear record of all transactions. I insisted on sharing and reviewing the daily expenses to avoid any misunderstandings and planned to share the total at the end of the trip. Sensing an odd tone, I told him I had sent all transaction details, and he should calculate it how he wanted and share it in the needed format. He replied, "I won't be doing all that." I couldn't shake the feeling that something suspicious might be on his mind.

This incident was another mood spoiler due to the way he talked to me. It would have been better if he explained what plan he had in mind for handling the expenses at the beginning of the trip. My aim was to make sure that everyone paid for their own expenses, avoiding any need for anyone to reimburse others.

Tip: Travel buddies need to establish ground rules for how expenses will be handled and settled during the trip.

For expenses like museum tickets or taxi rides, we can split the bill equally. I'll only pay for what I use. Sometimes, one person might pay for others, especially when we need coins for train tickets.

We had an early morning train to Venice. The train station was at a walking distance of 10-15 minutes. As we left the apartment, Annie found that the juice in the fridge had frozen. Since it was their beverage, I didn't really notice where it was placed. She didn't seem happy about it. We reached the station and boarded the train to Venice.

Tip: Ensure to wash the dishes before departing from the Airbnb. Airbnb also provides ratings for guests based on their cleanliness and behaviour.

One of the ways to enhance miles is to travel.

Chapter 7

Reflections on Sacrifice and Lessons Learned: Dealing with Ungrateful Friends

In Venice, we exited the train station, crossed the street, and took a bus to our hotel. The bus conductor suggested purchasing tickets from the shop across for a better price. The bus dropped us off 10 minutes away from our hotel. The weather was pleasant, not as hot as in Rome. Conveniently, there was a grocery store just at a walkable distance of 5 minutes from where we stayed.

When we got to the hotel, they wanted our passports. Annie gave photocopies and a police report, but they refused to accept it. They insisted on seeing an actual passport from at least one person staying with them.

Annie forgot that in Rome, I checked in and gave my passport at the reception while they waited in the lobby. In Venice, she realized the hotel wouldn't permit check-in without my passport. I quickly showed it to the hotel representative.

She indicated the room keys would be ready in 30 minutes. We settled into the lobby, occupying the large six-seater sofas with our luggage. My frustration had already been building due to Peter's behaviour in Florence and the incident at Michelangelo's viewpoint (sightseeing within 3-8 minutes). It got worse when Peter got impatient, pushing to start sightseeing immediately.

Travelers usually want to fully experience a city by sightseeing and enjoying the beauty of the place, instead of Peter's way of quickly moving between locations on trains or buses, just catching fleeting glimpses of attractions in about 3-8 minutes.

Peter urged us not to rest or freshen up before seeing the attractions, emphasizing to drop our bags and start sightseeing right then. However, later on: a) he complains of low energy, b) spends more time on buses en route to attractions, and c) rushes to leave most places within 5 minutes, with a maximum stay of 25 minutes at a few places. His fast-paced travel style – constant rush from one place to another can be tiring. This was the second time after Rome that Peter wanted to go sightseeing without resting. I was worried because if I didn't agree with him, it would cause problems. But if I did, and he got sick, Annie would talk a lot about staying healthy and cancelling plans, just like she did in Rome when we waited for the train to the Spanish Steps. I felt like they rushed things themselves and tried to pressurise me instead of fixing their attitude. Ultimately, it's really hard to deal with someone's negative attitude and emotional outbursts for a long time.

Seeking a change in atmosphere, I decided to call my friends and my mom while they waited in the lobby with our luggage.

While talking and walking, I noticed a coffee shop near the hotel entrance. Still on the phone, I went back to let them know about it in case they wanted coffee and snacks. Remembering Annie gets hungry around 1-2 PM, I showed concern for them and then went back to my call. I noticed they were sitting without intending to order. Being a coffee lover, I got a café latte for myself, as I'm used to managing my meals independently—a habit I established from the beginning.

As I sipped my coffee while chatting on the phone, and occasionally walked around, I noticed both of them looking my way unhappily. They got up, left their luggage, and headed in my direction. Ignoring their annoyed looks, I politely offered to keep an eye on their bags. I settled in the lobby with my coffee, continuing my phone conversation.

It didn't take me long to figure out that their annoyance stemmed from my decision to order coffee for myself without ordering any for them.

In Rome, they had low energy due to insufficient food intake, like having just half a burger as a meal. Given their age and daily walking, this was using up their energy quickly, which could have led to health concerns. To make sure they had a good meal, I treated them to a nice restaurant in Rome. However, doing it once didn't mean I had to continue for the entire trip.

Peter was eager to go sightseeing, so we decided to go out. Since it was raining, we decided to grab our jackets and an umbrella. When I went back to the lobby to get my umbrella from the luggage counter, I asked at the reception about our room. The receptionist gave us the room keys. I also carried the umbrella I bought for my sister in Amsterdam.

Annie had her jacket and a raincoat, and when we stepped outside, the rain got heavier. Peter didn't have anything, so Annie told him to get his jacket. I suggested he could rent an umbrella for 2 euros from the hotel, instead, he went back to the room to get his jacket, only to realize he left it in the hotel in Rome four days ago. After about 10 minutes, Annie called him. To our surprise, he admitted to losing his jacket and blamed Annie on the phone. She looked hurt. When I asked about packing, Annie explained they both pack bags independently, and Peter handles his packing because he likes it a certain way. Peter needed to take responsibility for forgetting the jacket instead of blaming his wife. It was unbelievable to see that he leaves no stone unturned to spoil the moods of his co-travellers.

His actions hinted at possible insecurities, suggesting a fear of his wife outshining him and potentially diminishing his importance. This might explain his tendency to dominate her and restricting her freedom to speak freely.

During our walk to the bus stop, I suggested to Peter that he should ask the hotel about his jacket because they often return lost items. He didn't like my suggestion and insisted he might have lost it on the train and not at the hotel. I still insisted that there was no harm in checking, but he rudely responded it wasn't at the hotel. His behaviour dampened the mood once again, so I decided to keep quiet. It was another lesson for me, seeing that he doesn't like advice, even when it could help him.

We got on the bus and headed to the harbor. When we got there, we asked about the price of gondola rides. Both Annie and I were interested. However, Peter insisted on taking a boat to the other side of the water to Canal Grande, assuring us we would do the gondola rides later. He didn't even allow us to take a photo with the gondola rides.

We bought tickets to cross the river. When we got on the boat, I saw them choosing seats by a window. I purposely sat on the other side, thinking about the uncomfortable touching gestures in Amsterdam and wanting the window seat for photos. Meanwhile, I noticed a guy taking pictures of his girlfriend from different angles. I asked him politely if he could take some pictures of me too. Before handing over my phone, I usually think about two things: a) if my phone is safe (being in the middle of the river meant it was secure, and nobody could run off with it), and b) if the person seems trustworthy. The guy took some excellent pictures of me.

Once we got to the other side, we strolled for about 10 minutes, passing fancy waterfront restaurants. Knowing Peter and Annie's usual concerns about cost, I checked if they were comfortable dining at one of the fancy restaurants. Peter enthusiastically agreed and even suggested taking a photo of Annie to post on Facebook. But for me, wanting to eat at a nice restaurant was more about personal enjoyment than showing it off to everyone.

Tip: Wait at least a week after coming back from your vacation before sharing photos on social media. Sharing them while you're still away is like letting burglars know there's no one at home and encouraging them to steal.

At Venice Costello, when the waiter asked for our food choices, Peter wanted me to convey to him to bring one pizza with an equal number of slices for all three of us. The waiter clarified we needed to order a minimum of two pizzas. I quietly excused myself to avoid any awkwardness. However, Peter misinterpreted and insisted the waiter get one pizza, thinking it would be enough for all of us. The waiter made a sarcastic comment, suggesting our order wasn't suitable for the restaurant, and recommended going to nearby lanes where we could buy individual pizza slices from street vendors. Peter thanked him, not realizing he was insulted. Annie and I stayed quiet.

As we ventured into the inner lane, we found a small Indian restaurant where an Indian salesperson enthusiastically promoted their cuisine. Knowing Peter's stingy nature, I thought this place might be more budget-friendly, so I asked him if they were open to the idea of dining there. He agreed, and we got a table with four seats. Peter asked if I wanted a Coke with the pizza, but I declined because of a sore throat. Any cold drinks would have worsened my throat's condition. When the waiter came, Peter tried to order one pizza with equal no of slices and one Coke. This waiter also said we had to order at least two pizzas. Worried about getting kicked out again, I swiftly intervened and said I'd have one whole pizza, and the couple could share the other one. It was 4 PM, and I was worried about their well-being since they only had tea and bhujiya in the morning.

I asked the waiter for complimentary water due to my sore throat, and he kindly provided it. The Coke was served, and the couple enjoyed their shared drink while I got busy with my mobile. When the pizza arrived, Annie finished her half Coke and politely requested her husband if she could have another one.

I was shocked to see Peter's reaction. He started scolding Annie for asking for another Coke, implying if she wanted a whole can of Coke, he could have ordered his beer, and she could have had the entire Coke to herself. Despite his displeasure, he eventually ordered another Coke to share between the two. When both pizzas were brought to the table, he commented about how they wouldn't be able to finish the pizzas and that one pizza would have been enough for the three of us. I chose to disregard his comment and relished the entirety of my pizza while they shared theirs. Despite his curiosity about me finishing a whole pizza, it was a satisfying meal for me.

After we ate, we hopped on another boat to cross the river to catch the bus to the hotel. The bus stop was crowded, so it was crucial to be careful not to lose things. Peter spotted a bus to our hotel and insisted we get on immediately. Sadly, our plans for the gondola rides were scrapped because Peter wasn't interested, and he didn't let any of us consider it. Venice is renowned for its gondola rides. Missing it felt like we missed out on something special.

I strongly believe if someone isn't willing to spend money on meals and attractions, they shouldn't embark on a foreign trip. On this trip, it was clear that Peter wanted things his way without considering what Annie and I wanted. I wasn't part of their family and had spent a lot of my hard-earned money to enjoy different attractions, but Peter's insensitivity and negative attitude ruined the experience for me. Unfortunately, I don't have any photos of the gondolas because of his behaviour.

Finally, we reached the hotel. I went straight to my room, but they were slower and arrived about 10 minutes later. They asked if I wanted something to eat, but I said I might skip a meal due to the throat infection, choosing liquids instead. Internally, I felt frustrated by Peter because he didn't let me take a gondola ride or enjoy attractions at my own pace. He always seemed in a rush to go and come back from places.

Consequently, I decided to distance myself from them and went to the lobby to call my family and friends to vent my frustration. I spent four hours there, drinking coffee, and even called a friend to wish her a happy birthday. I also used the time to calculate our expenses in euros since we were switching to Swiss francs in two days. I preferred not to start keeping track of a new currency. They noticed my four-hour absence, and when I returned, Peter said they reimbursed me for the train tickets and thanked me for helping during tough times. In response, I told them that there was no need for such formalities. I had a hunch that he paid because he worried I might leave midway through the trip, and they needed my passport as a kind of security.

The next day, Annie and Peter had breakfast early, and I joined them a bit later. We talked about our plan for the following day, wanting to catch a 7 am train to Milan by leaving at 5:30 AM. Peter was worried about missing breakfast, probably because of the extra cost.

I expressed leaving so early wasn't necessary since the train station wasn't far. But, as usual, he disagreed. I called a hostess and inquired if we could get a takeaway breakfast at 5:30 AM, and she agreed. If I had told Peter directly, he might have taken credit for the idea.

Tip: Always check with the hotel if they can pack food for you, especially if you are leaving early.

Around 10 AM, we revisited the same harbor, and once again, Peter insisted on going to Burano, known for its glass factory, instead of choosing a gondola ride. My toothache was still bothering me, so I didn't feel like talking much and kept quiet most of the time. I sat separately to avoid Peter and often asked fellow passengers to take pictures for me. At one point, while Peter was on a call, Annie offered to take my pictures.

Whenever she did, I ensured to confirm which shoulder she had trouble with before putting my purse on her shoulder. Although I considered my friend's needs, I couldn't help but feel that they weren't very sensitive to others, despite their age and life experience.

While Peter was busy on his phone, we took a quick look at some shops. When he finished his call, he instructed us to return to the hotel.

On the way back to the hotel, they decided to stop at a grocery store to get something to eat. I wasn't interested due to my toothache, so I went straight to the room. They returned without any food, explaining they couldn't find anything suitable to eat. Peter then mentioned they needed to buy a travel adapter. I reminded them that I already provided one, and we had determined the cost. I questioned the necessity of buying one for the remaining 5 days. Nonetheless, Peter said he wanted to find the cost and would be going to the market. The way he said it made it seem like he might be hiding something, perhaps going to eat without telling me. I had already expressed that I wasn't hungry and preferred to dine on my own, so I couldn't fathom the need for this little white lie.

Tip: Inquire at the hotel front desk if they have any adapters available for charging your phone.

An hour later, they returned and Peter said they got the adapter from the hotel and further revealed that his jacket was found in Rome, according to the receptionist downstairs. Since our current hotel was part of the same chain as the one in Rome, the receptionist contacted the Rome hotel to check on the jacket, but they instructed him to pick it up in person. I expressed that it was great news and suggested he inquire about having it shipped. In response, Peter raised his voice saying the hotel's policy wouldn't allow for shipping. I questioned if he checked with anyone, and he insisted he knew the hotel's policies. I was surprised that my efforts to help him get his jacket were met with a raised voice and policy assertions, especially without confirming with the hotel. Feeling frustrated, I decided to stay silent, thinking it was futile to discuss the matter further with someone who seemed uncooperative.

To let out my frustration, I left the room after a few minutes and went to the lobby to make a few phone calls. I vented to a friend about Peter's behaviour, mentioning how challenging it is to understand him. I had previously suggested Peter to ask the hotel about his missing jacket, but he didn't seem interested. Surprisingly, within 24 hours, he took my advice. My friend indicated he's the type of person who doesn't like to admit or give credit to others for their suggestions.

Annie's medicine helped with my toothache during the day, but I started feeling feverish. I called my mom for advice, worried that my trip could be ruined if I didn't get better. I asked her to pray for my health, and she suggested a medicine she had packed in a kit for me.

Before taking the medicine, I decided to have a meal and ordered focaccia. It was incredibly satisfying and delicious, with cheese, spinach, and a few other tasty ingredients. The portion was big, so heavy that two people could easily share it by splitting it in half. I thoroughly enjoyed savoring the whole focaccias. I highly recommend trying focaccia while in Italy.

Their small white lie came to light during one of our train journeys in Switzerland when Annie mentioned enjoying focaccia, and I realized that we both had focaccia at the same hotel, albeit at different times. The only difference was that they claimed they were going to the market for an adapter, but they were actually downstairs looking for a jacket, travel adapter, and dining. I had already said I couldn't eat due to a toothache, so their plans to dine in the lobby didn't interest me much anyway. The only difference is that in Rome when I dined in the lobby, I politely asked if they wanted to join.

Before going to bed, I took the medicine my mom recommended. It not only helped me sleep well but also contributed to my recovery by morning, completely eliminating my fever.

The next day, I thanked Annie for the medicine she gave me. I told her the one my mom suggested played a big part in making me completely better without any fever. I added that being a mother herself, she might understand the strength of a mother's prayers in these situations.

We picked up our takeaway breakfast and called a taxi. The station was close, just a 15-minute ride away. Once again, we arrived at the station an hour before the train's departure time. It looked like Peter didn't learn from the lost passport incident and didn't listen when I suggested leaving around 6:20 AM instead of 5:45 AM. Anyway, we were on our way.

Typically, when I travel alone, I consider the following:

A) For short train trips, like a 2-hour journey, I schedule the train for 11 AM and aim to leave around 10 AM from the hotel depending on the distance.

B) I enjoy a calm breakfast.

C) I make sure to take pictures in the hotel if I haven't already.

D) I book a cab ahead of time.

E) If I have an early train, I have the cab booked the night before through the hotel's reception. They need to make sure the cab comes on time because, with services like Uber, drivers can cancel at the last minute.

Peter once more appeared impatient because the platform number was not displayed, so I gently reminded him that platforms are usually assigned 30 minutes prior to departure. Given that it was a small train station, we waited.

Since we left Amsterdam, I intentionally chose seats on the opposite side of all the trains we boarded. Even on this occasion, when we got on the train, I sat on the opposite side. If they liked the left side, I sat on the right. Feeling hungry, I indulged in my takeaway breakfast with two croissants, a muffin, and juice. They opened one box and shared their meal. Sometimes, I noticed they explained why they were sharing, like Annie saying the croissants were heavy. I just smiled and focused on enjoying my meal, not worrying about what they were eating.

When we got to Milan, we had a connection to Lucerne, but the Lucerne train got cancelled. Peter looked frustrated, worrying about reaching Switzerland and the potential financial loss. He talked to Annie about two train options, one leaving at 11 AM and the other at 1 PM, insisting they must catch the 11 AM train no matter what. I stayed quiet for a while. I sensed Annie might not have liked my silence and passive behaviour, but I had my reasons.

Dealing with her husband's behaviour had become increasingly tough for me. Whenever I said something, he tended to do the opposite and argue loudly. To avoid getting upset, I often chose to stay silent. But on this occasion, I decided to break my silence and suggested that in the event of train cancelations, there might be a desk to help us rebook tickets, so we should attempt to locate it. Using my experience in the airline industry, I mentioned that when flights are cancelled for reasons beyond the customer's control, we usually rebook them on partner flights or reschedule for the next available one. I explained that trains often follow a similar practice, rebooking passengers on other trains or giving suitable alternatives in case of cancelations or disruptions.

Peter finally understood my point, and I asked a staff member in uniform about the desk's location. He directed us there and we found a long queue at the counter. It was evident that Peter had something on his mind, so I waited patiently to see how he would react. He instructed Annie to stand in a corner, and both Annie and I collectively decided to position ourselves where there was a closed door behind us to prevent anyone from coming from behind. After a few minutes, Peter returned and suggested that I stand in the line while he accompanied Annie. Suddenly I had a strong intuition that something was amiss and going on in his mind.

As my turn was coming up, Peter told me he would wait in line, and that I should go back to Annie. I complied with his request. After a few minutes, I asked him if he had my ticket, and he said, "No." This made me wonder if he was initially checking the train reservation only for himself and his wife. I questioned why he hadn't asked for my ticket and he had no answer. This situation revealed Peter's cunning nature, and it started to fuel my anger. I returned to Annie to voice my complaint.

Annie mentioned that in Amsterdam, I told her I had a printout of only my ticket to Lucerne. I also suggested to Annie and Peter to print their train tickets since they lost all the printouts due to theft. I agreed with her but insisted that it still didn't justify Peter standing in the queue to reschedule the cancelled train without my ticket. It strongly indicated he had no plans to get my ticket rescheduled.

Annie began to clarify that her husband wasn't like that. Suddenly, Peter called me, and when I looked at him, he used hand gestures to signal me to join him where he was standing. He then relayed that he talked to a representative who confirmed there was only one seat for the 11 AM train, so we had to book our tickets on the mobile app. He asked me to use one of the train apps. I was surprised by his behaviour because he was only thinking about himself. I firmly expressed I wasn't willing to buy a new ticket since the cancelation wasn't my fault, and it was the train company's responsibility to rebook me on the next available journey.

On one hand, I was thinking about Peter's statement, and a few things made me question it:

1. When he said, "They have one ticket for the 11 AM train, so we have to book our tickets," I wondered if he meant Annie could go alone on the available ticket, while he and I take the next train. It seemed he didn't plan on sending me with the available ticket because he suggested I should buy a new one. Also, his use of "our tickets" didn't include Annie.
2. He didn't even discuss this with his wife, which strongly suggested he might have hidden intentions. When he talked about two train options (11 AM and

1 PM) to Annie, he involved her in the decision-making process. However, when discussing booking the ticket through the app, he called me over from 8 feet away from the help desk instead of joining Annie and me where we were standing. This behaviour raised questions about why he chose not to include Annie in that particular conversation.

3. Typically, a gentleman would suggest in front of his wife that there's one ticket available, so the three of us could take the next train at 1 PM together.
4. Peter's intentions were clear at this point. It seemed he wanted to spend time alone with me by sending his wife alone on the available ticket. Since the Heineken incident, I had purposely kept some distance. So this situation might have looked like a golden opportunity to him.
5. If Peter were to present a printout of two tickets, the help desk agent would only process two PNRs. Given the long queue already present, it was unlikely that the agent would proactively consider working on my ticket when she didn't even have the PNR number for it. Surprisingly, Peter didn't even inquire about my ticket.

I acted quickly and went to the train representative, showing her my ticket and requesting her to consider it for rescheduling since she was already working on their tickets. She acknowledged she would help but also warned me to manage Peter because he had caused her a lot of stress and wasn't good at communicating. It wasn't surprising considering

Peter had been a source of stress for me since the beginning of our journey!

The representative further shared that Peter had requested a business class seat during the rebooking. I was taken aback and told her to assign me any available seat. I wasn't concerned about what he had requested for himself. In the end, she allocated two business class seats and one economy class seat on the first available train. I was really happy to be in a different carriage, away from them for a while.

At that particular moment, I chose not to comment on the matter of the business and economy class seats because Peter's behavior had been causing irritation within me. I wanted to assess how far he would go in this situation. This incident served as a reality check for me, showing that a) he would have been fine leaving me behind to prioritize their own journey, and b) if he was willing to disclose information about the business class seats himself.

This incident left me feeling a bit foolish for sacrificing my own plans to stay with them when they lost their passports in a foreign country. I was considerate, thinking they are older, and should be comfortable. I never questioned their choices and always went along with what they wanted to do. However, it made me wonder if Peter had forgotten my help. It reminded me that some people can be forgetful and ungrateful.

Since the representative had documented and stamped the details on my ticket, I asked Annie to take a photo of it to show to the train checker. After that, we found the train and boarded.

I boarded the train first as my compartment was located near the front. Their compartment was at the back of the train.

My compartment was exceptionally nice and spacious. I had a seat by the window and sat across from a tall man working on his laptop. My seat faced the door to the next compartment, which looked like scenes we often see in English movies—a setup like a restaurant with two-seater tables, four-seater tables, and a standing room near the bar.

The entire setup enticed me to leave my seat and go sit in that area. So, I grabbed my bags and made myself comfortable there. I ordered a snack and a cappuccino and relished my "Me time."

The train journey lasted for three hours. Annie kindly texted me to see if I had settled, and I replied with a simple "Yes". At the next stop, I messaged Annie that it was our station, and she responded with a thumbs-up. I disembarked and waited for them to join me on the platform outside my compartment.

When they got there, an elderly English couple bid them farewell, and Peter engaged in a pleasant conversation with them. It was the third time I saw Peter being remarkably polite to strangers. On the flip side, I had consistently noticed that Annie's interactions with people remained fairly standard and didn't vary much based on the individuals' backgrounds. However, with Peter, it appeared he was polite and amiable with everyone external except for those he was with, whether it was his family, friends, or his wife's friends.

After the elderly couple left, Peter's first question was, "Did you eat something?" I couldn't help but find it amusing how focused he was on my eating habits. I shared what I had eaten and my delightful experience in the train's bar and restaurant. Peter commented, "You should have called me, and I would have come to eat in the restaurant." He was okay with getting a call from me if I was having a meal, but he wasn't willing to send a text informing me about business class seats and offering to swap seats to accompany Annie and give the girls some time together. This clearly demonstrated his selfishness.

Annie, in her excitement and innocence, revealed that they were seated in business class, opposite the two elderly passengers they had talked to. This disclosure left Peter quiet, as he had been under the impression that I wasn't aware of the business class seats. It raised my eyebrows as this was the second time in less than 4 hours that he hinted at leaving Annie behind and being alone with me for a meal. It all seemed rather weird. Clearly, he would have instructed Annie to watch over the bags since he mentioned 'You should have called me, and I would have joined you'.

We searched for the next train platform, and the journey to Lucerne's main station took less than 30 minutes. The scenic view from the train included mountains and a lake, and we finally reached the main station.

No guaranteed card comes with relations.

Chapter 8

Disagreement between Co-travellers

At last, we reached the train station, and at that point, Peter put his trust in Google Maps to guide us to the hotel. Despite my doubts about the accuracy of his Google Maps directions, we followed him as he made a left turn. I was worried because he hadn't checked the hotel address, and there could be several hotels with the same name under this brand. To clear my doubts, I suggested to Annie that we call the hotel for guidance. I dialled the hotel's number and put the phone on speaker mode.

The receptionist told us we were going the wrong way; the hotel wasn't nearby. Instead, she told us to catch a bus from a specific stop, just a 10-minute ride from where we were. We found the bus stop and reached the hotel without any problems. While checking in, the receptionist asked about city taxes. To keep transactions clear, especially since the currency was no longer in euros, I asked her to charge one tax on my card. I assured her that the others in our group would pay their taxes separately. They did, and in return, the receptionist gave us the room keys as agreed.

After checking in, I prepared to explore the local sights alone. I went to Annie and said, "I've kept the adapter and wire to charge your phones and watch first, and I'll use a power bank in the meantime. I'd like to explore attractions since we're in Switzerland, and you don't need my passport or me anymore as you would receive your white passports the next day."

Annie said "What you would have heard about our community, we are not like that".

I replied "I don't have any friends from your community besides you, so I haven't heard anything. I'm not sure what you're talking about" even though I understood she was implying that their community is considered thrifty or stingy with money.

Suddenly, Peter reacted and said, "She doesn't want to pay for our hotel tax now."

I replied "It's not like that; given that Swiss Francs are used in Switzerland, not euros, there was no need to track expenses in Swiss francs as long as we paid for own expenses independently. Consequently, I notified the receptionist that I would personally cover my hotel tax."

Peter said "Annie, she doesn't want to be with us: she doesn't even share her meals, she wouldn't even like to eat with us or will do breakfast with us tomorrow."

I responded "Both of you consistently spoke in your language whether on the road, in hotels, restaurants, boats, or elsewhere. About 98% of your communication was in your language, with only 2% in Hindi or English when I specifically asked something. This behaviour suggests exclusion. Also, I'm paying for my own meal, I prefer to enjoy a full and satisfying meal, especially given that I'm walking throughout the day."

Annie supported Peter "Our regional language is a simple language to understand".

I responded "I really don't understand your language, it's generally expected that people communicate in a language everyone understands. In a work setting, we make sure not to speak in our language when there are foreign clients. It's a simple courtesy to talk in a language that everyone in the room understands."

Peter said "Agree, it's our fault and we didn't realise, we should have been careful".

It was strange that during the whole trip, they spoke in their language, but when the blame or mugging incident occurred, they switched to a language we all understood. This made me wonder if it was done on purpose to include me or not.

Peter said, "You even sat on other side of the boat in Venice and not with us."

I mentioned, "I decided to sit on the opposite side of the boat to enjoy the view and take pictures of the attractions for my family. Initially, you only needed my help until you got your passports, and now we're in the country where you can get them."

Peter said "Annie, now she doesn't want us to take her pics and ask others to take her pics,"

I replied, "I prefer strangers taking my photos because sometimes when you take pictures, my head or the background of the sightseeing gets cut off, and you tend to take photos quickly. For example, compare the pictures I took of Leaning Tower of Pisa without anyone in the background—perfect for framing on the living room wall—to the one you took with people in the background. That's why I choose to have strangers take my pictures; they are more willing to listen to how I want the photo and the preferred angle."

I also said, "Has he noticed how he talks to me rudely compared to how politely he addresses strangers with 'thank you, sir' and 'thank you, ma'am'? When talking to Annie and me, he treats us differently. I want to emphasize that I'm not a family member; I'm just an outsider and a friend. I expect to be spoken to respectfully, and if he wants to use a harsh tone, then he can talk to his wife, as they are married."

He said 'We felt you were upset because we didn't transfer money for train tickets, so we transferred it'

I responded 'I'm not money minded, and a self-made individual but don't appreciate being spoken to rudely. I never asked for money for train tickets, understanding that you've had financial setbacks. As a self-made person without a spouse or kids, my main joy is international travel. I might not be as affluent as you, and I invested lakhs in this trip to experience attractions. However, what you've shown me is just an 8-minute view of Florence, 20 mins of view of Leaning Tower of Pisa. Is that how we're supposed to appreciate an attraction?"

Continuing I added "I joined this trip to explore attractions, but a brief eight-minute view of Florence, followed by a rushed departure for a bus in Pisa, doesn't match my idea of experiencing them. As a solo traveller, I enjoy international travel, investing 4-5 lakhs annually. Hurrying through sightseeing isn't my preference, so maybe it's best for each of us to pursue our own interests in Switzerland."

Annie said, "We asked you if you wanna go to this attraction or not and most of the time you said neutral".

I responded "I agreed to visit any attraction, but my concern is leaving a place within 3-8 minutes, like Florence view, which left me unsatisfied. Since I've spent not in thousands but in lakhs, and travel is my main source of joy as an unmarried person, it fills a void in my life that has now been spoiled. I can't travel repeatedly to see the same attraction. If you slept in the afternoon and the delay in going to attractions with the desire to return early doesn't work for me."

I further added, "When trip happens you ask the choices of everyone. On previous trips, when I traveled to Europe with my sister and a friend, we had dedicated each day for one of us. Despite being in the majority with my sister, we ensured our friend never felt out of place. In contrast, on this trip, you are also in majority but making every effort to make me out of place like talking in your language, doing only what Peter wants, likes or how he wants to do things."

Annie said, "You could have asked to lead".

I responded "In a trip, there can't be two leaders, where did he give an opportunity. When I suggest anything, he starts scolding or does opposite. For instance, when I proposed asking the hotel about the lost jacket and the option of having it couriered, Peter's response was harsh, emphasizing policies. If my suggestions bother you, I will stay silent. I was genuinely concerned that you don't have another loss". He ignored my statement and changed the topic.

Peter mentioned that "We got stuck in Rome and with the assistance of that lady we reached hotel so for safety concerns he mentioned to abandon the Florence view."

Annie supported Peter by adding "In Rome, we got stuck at underground metro when no cabs were available".

I said, "It was an unusual situation similar to Amsterdam mugging and it was my efforts that I spoke to the lady and got us out of the situation."

Suddenly, my phone rang, Annie now became the situational leader and said, "Ok whatever has happened, let's forget that we will now see what you want to see."

Oddly, at the Colosseum, Peter first planned to buy a 40 euro ticket for fast access, but later proposed independent exploration and meeting at a specific spot. Ironically, when I asked to explore on my own, they objected. The decision to meet at a designated time seemed to be more in line with their convenience.

I stepped away to make a call and went to the lobby. I spoke to the receptionist, asking about reaching the city centre and learning about local attractions. The receptionist informed me that Lucerne offers free Wi-Fi, shared the code, and highlighted that it's just a 4-minute train ride to the central station from the hotel.

Annie and Peter joined too so I relayed the information.

En route to the train station, Annie and I walked side by side. She remarked, "The trip wasn't that bad? You could have intervened and stopped us from speaking in our language, as some of our other friends had advised against using our native language in the past."

I expressed, "It's generally expected that people use a language everyone can understand. I didn't intervene as a sign of respect for senior citizens. Your friends might stop you because they are around your age, but being much junior to you, I was reluctant to tell you. I can't say anything to your husband but express it to you, the train representative shared that Peter caused her a lot of stress during the reservation process, and I've faced similar stress dealing with him."

I mentioned, "I helped you through the tough times of the lost passport. But, during the rescheduling of train tickets, he stood in the line without my ticket. Despite having a reservation for one ticket, he asked me to book my own train, a clear intention of wanting me to be left behind".

Annie mentioned, "She knows her husband, and he would never leave you in such a situation. You only mentioned that you had a printout of your ticket, and we printed our tickets at the hotel."

I mentioned, "Yes, I did suggest you print your ticket, but it doesn't justify why he stood in the queue with both yours and his tickets without asking for mine. This incident served as a reality check for me. My family has advised me not to travel with anyone's husband or brother in the future."

Annie supported her husband by stating "My husband wouldn't leave anyone behind."

I mentioned, "If there was only one ticket available, shouldn't he involve you in the discussion? His response should have been that three tickets aren't available together, and we could book next train departing at 1 PM. Also, hotels typically don't allow check-in before the afternoon or, in some cases, by 4 PM."

Annie again supported her husband by stating "He isn't like that. I know my husband."

I mentioned, "While your husband shares with all his relatives about the embassy guy assistance, he has never mentioned my name, despite the fact that I was the one who introduced the contact."

She stated, "My husband shared your name with all our relatives, acknowledging your help with the embassy contact, and I personally witnessed it."

I replied, "Okay, I believe your word. But every time I try to engage in conversation with someone, he consistently interrupts, as seen with the lady I spoke to in Rome who arranged the cab; he also tends to take credit for such situations."

Annie remarked, "Peter is impulsive and doesn't listen, often interfering and blaming others for his mistakes. He prefers taking credit over acknowledging others. Unfortunately, he's unable to change his nature. Similarly, just as you're filled with complaints, he too is filled up to the neck with it."

I mentioned, "But what did I do? I never complained; I remained silent and followed where you wanted to go. On the contrary, your husband sometimes complains and remarks that we visit every Monday bazar. After all, we've come overseas to explore attractions and shops. The designs of clothes in a foreign country are different from what we have in our home country. If we don't engage in sightseeing or shopping, then what's the point of traveling overseas? He mentioned that I had said "Euro to Euro.""

Annie replied, "Considering your prior mention that Indian currency would be settled in INR and euros in euros, Peter aimed to balance the expenses. So, the amount you spent on train tickets for all of us due to lost passport, he intended to offset it with expenses like tickets to attractions, trains, or buses."

I was taken aback by this revelation but concealed my emotions. I responded, "I hadn't intended to spend that much in such a short time. We were almost break even in euros. Additionally, offsetting Euro transactions with Swiss currency seemed illogical due to different conversion rates. Just as Euro transactions are settled in Euro, Swiss Franc transactions should be settled in Swiss Francs. We would have to start tracking expenses in Swiss currency, so it's best if we pay for our own expenses using Swiss currency. Moreover, given that my credit card incurred the conversion charges for all the train reservations, it would be appropriate to settle those in INR since those transactions were not mine."

I'm not sure if Peter and Annie thought the Euro and Swiss currency were the same because the Schengen visa is the same for both, but they are actually different currencies, and their conversion rates are different too.

It did make me wonder why they didn't use their card perhaps it was to avoid incurring conversion charges.

I sought clarification regarding Peter's comment, "She (Rebecca) keeps sending a daily account, and we should total everything and divide by three."

Annie remarked, "He thinks you have separate meals, and they assumed we would handle expenses similar to a domestic trip. I've realised that you operate differently, and we operate differently."

I replied, "I eat my entire meal because I dislike people eating from my plate with their used spoons. I need to stay healthy and energetic on a foreign land, so I eat complete meals."

I didn't comprehend her remarks about expenses during domestic trips, I refrained from commenting. It was only after returning to my home country, that I understood. I spoke with some married friends, and most of them shared that they usually pool a certain amount of money for expenses when traveling together, and one person holds the money for buying things like water, food, drinks, etc.

Now, this realization hit me even more because:

1. I recollected a domestic trip where Annie had requested a 2k contribution from each participant for food and taxi expenses. She held onto their money and covered all the expenses from that pool. Being relatively inexperienced in domestic travel and on my first trip with married women, I didn't oppose this rule due to societal norms. However, in my other travel experiences, both domestic and international with single women, we always settled our bills individually at the table without any discomfort or conflicts.

2. In international trips, you often pay six times more for items or meals compared to your home country. Given the diverse choices in food and sightseeing, it's challenging to split expenses equally. The only costs that could be shared are bus or train tickets.

3. Taking an upfront payment for daily expenses would imply covering the cost of Peter's two daily beers, signalling a desire to enjoy leisure at someone else's cost.

4. The rule for upfront payment should be communicated to travellers before the trip begins, not in the final stages of the journey. I had no prior knowledge of their expectations, as they continued making assumptions.

It seemed like they didn't grasp the difference between a national and an international trip.

On the train to the city center, Annie brought up that Peter feels excluded when we talk. I clarified that our discussions during the trip have been brief, and sometimes, they revolve around subjects better suited for women without necessarily requiring a man's involvement.

Upon reaching the main station, Chapel Bridge was close by, we strolled briefly and took some pictures. Once can easily walk from Chapel Bridge to Old Town. Peter suggested cycling as a way to make amends or please me, but I declined, indicating my disinterest.

For lunch, I suggested a nice restaurant at the beginning of the street. Annie wanted to explore more, but considering their budget-conscious approach, I recommended checking prices and vegetarian options before settling in a restaurant. We finally chose one, and I ordered chicken pasta, while they shared a vegetarian pizza and a beer. The bill came to 52 euros, and I asked the waiter to deduct 26 euros for my pasta, leaving them to cover the rest for their pizza and beer directly.

The Lion Monument, Lake Lucerne, and the Old Town were in close proximity, and after exploring them, we returned to the hotel.

In the evening, I inquired about Peter's decision regarding his jacket, and he said the hotel wouldn't courier it. I proposed having the hotel cover the courier charges, but he didn't give a clear response. Suddenly, he mentioned calling the hotel to connect with any Indian guest who could bring the jacket back to India, with plans to coordinate later. I prioritized charging their phones and watches using my cable and adapter. I made sure their devices were fully charged before charging my own phone in the middle of the night.

Next morning, our first stop was the embassy to collect the white passports. On the way, Peter bought few clothes for himself. Afterward, we rode a cable car to Mount Pilatus, reaching its highest point, featuring a restaurant and souvenir shops. Around the restaurant, there was snow, creating a beautiful backdrop for photos and exploration. The couple chose to stay indoors, while I ventured outside to enjoy the scenic views.

While taking selfies, I spotted another solo female traveller from Malaysia doing the same. I proposed taking each other's photos, and we spent 15 minutes together. As we climbed more stairs, our conversation made the walk enjoyable, and time flew by. The experience at Mount Pilatus was delightful. Upon returning to where they were waiting, Annie shared they had coffee at the restaurant, and I learned the tram would arrive in 5 minutes. With my habit of collecting souvenirs, I quickly explored the shops, informing Annie and Peter that I would be back shortly. In that short shopping trip, I bought a Swiss bell.

Peter and Annie had already used their tickets to swipe on the turnstile and were in line awaiting incoming tram. After my return, I swiped my ticket and rejoined them. I showed Annie the souvenir, piquing her interest to have similar item. But Peter insisted I go back to the shop and buy another for Annie. Returning meant purchasing another ticket at the turnstile, and with the tram about to arrive, it would have been more practical for him to buy something for his house if he desired it. This situation revealed a hint of selfishness.

After the tram ride, we took a train back to our hotel. Peter appeared anxious and began frantically checking his pockets. Curious, I asked if something was amiss. Peter revealed that he had lost his credit card, blaming his wife for misplacing it after he handed it to her to buy coffee. I inquired if they had any other cards.

He mentioned having two credit cards – one lost, and the other requiring a currency top-up. When I asked about Annie's cards, he indicated she had none. I suggested checking his email for the lost card's transaction history and contacting the corresponding shop, as people often return lost cards. Given he had only made two transactions that morning, I felt confident he would locate it. I witnessed him taking my advice for the first time and calling the restaurant where they had coffee, the last place he used his card. The lady at the restaurant verified that the card was found and agreed to send it from the mountains to the ticket booth where we took the cable car. Peter confirmed with the operator to pick it up the next day. While Peter was engrossed in the conversation, I observed tears in Annie's eyes as she gazed out the train window.

After concluding his call, Peter engaged in self-talk, pondering whether the card might be at the coffee counter. He assured himself that he would recover it the next day, bringing comfort. I couldn't help but remark, "Peter, you not only pinpointed the issue but also proposed a solution. I've observed this pattern throughout the trip where you state a problem and quickly propose a resolution in the next sentence on numerous occasions."

I couldn't help but ask Peter why he hadn't made his wife financially independent.

Peter responded, stating, "I gave her $1000 when she went on an international trip with her friends."

I responded, "You did this to ensure she could return home and take care of your family, so you gave her money as a safeguard."

Peter mentioned, "I'm with her, so she doesn't need money. I'm married to her and look after her needs"

I replied, "If this is you call marriage then I'm glad I'm not married, You should ensure her financial independence, whether you're with her or not."

Peter remarked, "You're taking a feminist stance, so you'll speak in favor of women."

I replied, "It's not about being feminist. The worry is that Annie isn't financially independent. She lacks a credit card or funds from you. In emergencies or for personal needs, she has to wait and consult you. If a train door closes or a stampede happens how would she reach you without an international number?"

Watching Annie smile after someone stood up for her, I added, "Considering all she does for the family, she truly deserves financial independence. It's liberating to manage finances independently without explaining every expense to someone else."

Peter mentioned, "I understand and agree with your point, both about my pattern of discussing problems and solutions, and on the topic of women's financial independence and you are right."

Annie mentioned she needed to use the restroom and excused herself. I advised Peter, "Now that you've realized, how about treating her to a candlelight dinner or giving her a gift? Small gestures can bring joy to a homemaker, and she deserves a special moment with you."

Peter said "I have given her everything at home"

I remarked, "Even if you've given her everything, at least treat her to a nice lunch or dinner."

Peter nodded and conversation ended.

Annie returned from restroom and sat beside me. Given Peter's prior lapse in not carrying my ticket during a cancelled train, I hesitated to rely on them for any reservations. As they had arranged the last hotel a day before our departure, I inquired about the details of the hotel reservation. Annie said, "No, not yet. I need to follow up." I requested, "Could you share the hotel confirmation?" to which she replied, "Yes."

On our way back to hotel, we stopped for dinner at McDonald's. I used a vending machine to order nuggets and coffee, while they opted for a small burger split in half and a large Coke.

At 9 PM, Annie and I finalized the attractions we wished to visit, and Peter didn't object. I was delighted that the itinerary for the next two days included the attractions I was excited about: the Yash Chopra statue at Kursaal Garden, Jungfrau, a jet boat ride on Lake Brienz, and a toy train ride. Choosing this plan helped alleviate some of the discomfort I faced earlier in the trip.

They put their phones and watches on the charger, while I charged mine in the middle of the night.

The next day, Peter went to get his credit card, and Annie and I went shopping. Peter later called Annie, saying he found the credit card at the coffee counter, as told by the cable ticket counter staff. Seeing Annie upset, she shared with me that Peter was blaming her. Unfortunately, Peter continued to affect his wife's mood negatively.

- The ticket counter person didn't witness the credit card discovery as it was sent by the coffee shop lady on the mountain.

- Knowing Peter's frugality, it seemed unlikely he'd forget to ask his wife for the credit card if he had given it to her.

- Annie vividly remembered handing the card to Peter.

- During our travels, it was consistently Peter misplacing passports, dropping the credit card at Amsterdam Central Station, and leaving his jacket at the hotel.

We returned to hotel, checked out and reached the main station to catch the train to Interlaken. With some time before boarding, Annie decided to grab lunch for both of them while Peter and I kept an eye on the bags. When she came back, I got a big salad bowl packed with eggs, kidney beans, corn, and various other ingredients.

We boarded the train and I suggested they should file a claim with their travel insurance, as it might offer recovery and potential compensation benefits. Peter said "I've already considered it and will be doing that".

Traveling serves as a reality check for relationships, revealing aspects of compatibility, communication, and mutual support.

Chapter 9

Heated Arguments

While on the train, Annie and I sat by the windows facing each other, and Peter took the aisle seat next to Annie. Even though Peter and Annie had their packed food, I wasn't hungry, so I enjoyed the scenic views and took some photos. The sight of Lake Brienz was breathtaking, and Peter suggested we could alight/get off, explore the lake, and store our luggage in lockers. However, despite our agreement, he didn't make efforts to get down so we remained silent. I felt, Peter says things without actually intending to follow through.

Annie shifted to a window seat on the other side of the train, enjoying the lake view, while it was lunchtime for me at 1 PM. Peter, curious about my meal, asked about its ingredients. Feeling a bit awkward with the scrutiny, I confirmed that it contained eggs and indirectly declined to share. I then inquired about the hotel booking, and Peter, claiming to have forwarded it before the journey. I checked and confirmed not receiving it. Upon verifying, he admitted that he hadn't shared it with me. As Annie was seated across the aisle, she wasn't aware of our conversation.

Upon reaching Interlaken, we went to the resort where the receptionist mentioned that check-in would take an additional hour and a half. Peter proposed leaving our bags at the reception and exploring the attractions. I decided to change clothes. The receptionist guided Annie and me to the changing room near the swimming pool area.

After changing, I asked Annie for her opinion on my outfit. Surprisingly, she replied, "I'm not your mother to tell you what to wear." Her response caught me off guard, and I felt she might be silently hurt. It seemed she was stuck between my comments and her husband's behaviour, likely frustrated by the conflict. We returned to lobby. As Annie and Peter got into a discussion, I approached the receptionist to arrange luggage storage. She mentioned we needed to return by 8 PM since they close, and no one would be available for keys afterward. She also informed us about the self-serve option for getting food at night from their in-house paid self-service shop.

I relayed the updated information to them. Annie mentioned changing our itinerary to visit Lake Thun that day, seeking my approval. I noticed Annie aligning with her husband's preference for the change, overlooking our past 19 days of following Peter's plan. Despite our recent conflict within the last 48 hours and our initial agreement for the day's plan to include Lake Brienz and Harder Kulm, Annie made changes without consulting me. Instead, she favored her husband by discussing the changes proposed by Peter amongst themselves while I was occupied with the receptionist. Among the three of us, Annie and Peter formed the majority. It was evident that whatever decision Peter made, Annie would support him blindly, leaving me to default to Peter's choice. My voice had depleted due to coughing hence I refrained from voicing objections. Communicating concerns through sign language posed a challenge.

Following Peter's directions, we reached a bus stop and boarded the bus. Peter told us where to go, and we found a bus stop. Finding seats, Annie and Peter sat together, while I sat across from them. Annie placed her crossbody bag on her lap after taking it off her neck. About 20 minutes later, Peter said our stop was next. Annie followed Peter, accidentally dropping her purse on the floor. I promptly picked it up and alerted her about the oversight. Relieved that she hadn't lost her purse, she exited the bus joyfully, and we disembarked.

After the bus left, Peter checked Google Maps and discovered that we had alighted at the wrong stop, with 45 minutes remaining to reach Lake Thun. The road was not heavily trafficked, and Peter confirmed that the next bus would arrive in 29 minutes. Despite my attempts to hitch a lift for the three of us, it proved unsuccessful. The bus eventually arrived, and we reboarded, selecting different seats based on availability. When Peter suggested getting off, so we did. With my voice depleted, I refrained from making suggestions because Peter tended to alter the agreed agenda or assert his preferences, without considering others' opinions.

We got off the bus again and didn't find the lake. Peter consulted Google Maps, and since I couldn't talk, I suggested through sign language to ask a local. Peter approached an elderly couple, and they confirmed that we were two stops ahead of Lake Thun.

By 6 pm, it seemed impractical to continue searching for Lake Thun, especially considering we hadn't obtained our room keys yet, and the reception would close at 8 pm. Annie and I both agreed to return to the hotel via the nearby train station instead of bus.

The first day at Interlaken got messed up as Peter led us to the wrong bus stops while attempting to find Lake Thun. I didn't express that the changes to the plan made us lose an entire day.

Upon arriving at the resort, we completed the check-in process. The apartment was fantastic, featuring a bedroom, kitchen, a bed in the living room, and a spacious balcony. What excited me the most was having a separate toilet and bathing area. It felt like my wish for two different spaces was finally granted. This was especially meaningful since, for over two weeks, Peter and Annie used the bathroom first for activities like using the toilet, brushing teeth, etc., would often cause delays when I wanted to take a shower.

We settled in the kitchen dining area. They indulged in some Indian snacks, bhujiya, and tea, while I opted for green tea from in-house available sachet. Although they offered me some bhujiya, I generally refrain from consuming anything related to India or Indian food on international trips when staying in hotels or resorts. It helps me feel like I'm abroad rather than in my home country.

I got a call from a friend, so I decided to go to the lobby for some privacy. Peter said they will go to their room and I could continue the conversation in the living room, but I still insisted on going to the lobby.

As I headed for the door, Peter kept his hand on my right shoulder to stop me, and said I can't go and should talk in the apartment. I was shocked to see his behaviour and screamed in my whatever voice I had left with to let me go and talk, but he didn't remove his hand not allowing me to step out. In the end, I requested Annie to step in and ask him to release his grip on me as I needed privacy for calls. When Annie intervened then only Peter removed his hand off my shoulder and I was relieved to come out of room.

As travellers, everyone should understand that little space is required amongst them. It's obvious that all the travellers will be sharing their good and bad experience with their family and friends. When you're upset with someone's behaviour, taking some private time to vent or cry can be essential. It's challenging to express those emotions in front of them since they are the reason you are upset. Venting privately helps release those emotions and prevents those frustrated feelings from building up inside.

After finishing my calls, I inquired with the receptionist about the routes to Schilthorn 007 and the trains from Interlaken to Zurich. I learned that there were trains with stops and direct options. I requested a printout of the train numbers and timings, noting that there was an hourly train to Zurich and a direct one every two hours.

I returned to the room. Annie and Peter were already ready, so we agreed to venture out to explore restaurants. Along the way, we saw the Victoria Hotel hosting an upscale corporate event. Intrigued, we entered the hotel, took some photos, and then continued on. Eventually, we settled on McDonald's for dinner. I ordered a Happy Meal with fish and nuggets, while they shared a staple item, splitting one burger between the two of them.

When my meal arrived in a large paper bag with mini boxes, they had already finished half of their burgers. My meal included a fish burger, a mixed juice, an apple juice, french fries, and 6 pieces of nuggets. Peter expressed interest in trying the french fries, and I nodded in agreement. As I was taking out the boxes of nuggets and the fish burger from paper bag, one of the boxes fell, coincidentally when he asked if he could try the fries. I sensed Annie might think I did it on purpose, but it wasn't intentional. While I enjoyed my meal, Peter kept glancing at my food or juice bottles, his intention unclear. Once I had eaten everything I ordered, he asked, "pait bgar gaya, kuch aur laon tumhaare liye (Is your stomach full? Do I get something more for you?") I politely declined, finding his statement a bit awkward, considering I was covering my own meal expenses throughout the trip and had taken a sufficient meal for dinner. I found his statement came off as sarcastic, implying that I had eaten a substantial or hearty meal and hadn't offered them any. I hold the perspective that if someone is hungry, they have the option to purchase their own meal rather thank looking at others meal.

On our way back, we stopped at Kursaal Park near our hotel and took photos with the Yash Chopra statue. The statue, symbolizing Yash Chopra as the ambassador of Interlaken, filled me with a sense of pride. Unfortunately, the pictures didn't turn out well due to the darkness. Anticipating that Peter and Annie might not want to return next day for more photos, I decided to revisit the site the next morning after breakfast.

The separation of toilet and bathing rooms allowed me to shower first, a change from days when they prioritized getting ready ahead of me. Deliberately allocating a brief time for my personal activities while they prepared to get ready, I aimed to avoid delays for my fellow travellers. This allowed me to fulfill my plan of going to Kursaal Park for a morning walk, enjoying the park's beauty, and capturing some good pictures as photos in sunlight turn out better than those taken in the late evening. I was conscious that if they had readied themselves first, my planned activities would have faced hindrances. After returning to the hotel, I enjoyed breakfast and cherished my daily routine of talking to my mom and friends during that time. Expressing frustrations and sharing stress with family and friends is a common human need. In such moments, having personal space becomes essential for venting and maintaining well-being.

I recall Annie sharing her frustration about taking the underground train and losing balance on an escalator in Brussels with her family and friends, who were empathetic. Like Annie, I also needed to vent my frustrations to my family and friends about our situation but chose not to do it in front of them to avoid causing discomfort.

Annie and Peter joined. Although Peter wanted to share my table, Annie stepped in, acknowledging my ongoing call, and suggested they find a separate table to give me some space. After finishing my breakfast, I approached their table, informing them that I would be waiting in the lobby while they finished eating. At the front desk, I asked for directions to Schilthorn 007 attraction for breakfast and other recommended places. The lady mentioned that on the return journey from Jungfrau, we will reach Lauterbrunnen, and there's a must-visit charming small town called Murren, and suggested combining it with the 007 attraction for next day. I made up my mind of seeing both

Mureen and Schilthorn whether they do it or not. I thanked her and quickly went to Kursaal Park, took pictures with Yash Chopra's statue in the daylight, and the photos turned out great.

We met in the lobby and set off for Jungfrau Mountain, a picturesque location featured in many of Yash Chopra's films. To reach Jungfrau, we had to change trains a few times from Grindelwald and other stops. It was a full-day excursion. After buying our separate tickets, we waited at Grindelwald for the train, and the train journey lasted around 1 hour and 45 minutes. I was struck by the map covers on all the tables inside the train, depicting the entire Jungfrau region, nearby areas, and routes to Lauterbrunnen. I found it to be incredibly impressive and imaginative. I quickly took the picture of the table so that it comes handy for my next day's trip to Schilthorn to see 007 sight. On the way to Jungfrau, the train made stops for photo opportunities and transfers.

Tip: Take note of any memorable experiences or insights on your phone or a paper napkin to add them to your to-do list, allowing you to relive those moments later on.

Once at Jungfrau, we decided to pursue our individual interests, planned to reunite at a specific time. Jungfrau was a unique experience, a location often found in Yash Chopra Movies like Chandani, there was wall on ice floor, one has to hold the railing to avoid a fall. After exploring, lunch, and buying souvenir, we hopped on the train for the return trip.

Tip: When choosing souvenirs, think about things like photos, postcards, ticket stubs, and maps from your trip. They're free and have sentimental value.

On the return train, I was happy with the positive experiences of the day. Engaging in conversation with Annie, I reminded exploring Harder Kulm for a panoramic view of Interlaken which Annie and I had already agreed in Lucerne. Abruptly, Peter interjected with an irritated tone, dismissing the idea by claiming that "all city offers same view". I felt like questioning him why is he traveling, and should have stayed at home, but I kept quiet. His comment made me think whether I should convey that not every conversation needs criticism. His unnecessary intrusion brings down the mood for everyone. I decided to remain silent. Neither I would talk nor I would have to listen to his irritating tone or comments and could keep my mood positive.

By 3 pm, we arrived at Lauterbrunnen station and Peter suggested visiting Murren another picturesque town and highlighted that Schilthorn is nearby, Now, how do I explain to Peter that Schilthorn is located on a mountain, and the only way to reach it is via cable, not by road. His intention implied that since he showed Schilthorn from a distance; there would be no further need to re-visit. However, I wasn't willing to miss out on the experience, especially during my last 36 hours of the trip. I remained silent.

We leisurely walked around, appreciating the town's beauty. I was pleased that I could visit Murren, originally planned for the next day. Annie mentioned that Peter committed to returning here with the kids within the next six months. I wondered why he wants to revisit and waste money when he can't stick to the plan, rushes through places, and doesn't fully appreciate our current trip's beauty.

Later, Peter said we had technically reached Schilthorn by walking, and since 007 was close, we could mark it as done. In my thoughts, I felt Peter was guiding me through the roads, not realizing that the 007 site is actually five mountains away and you need a cable car from the Schilthorn station. I knew he wouldn't be eager to spend on either the cable car or breakfast, both costing 100 Swiss Francs per person. Although I stayed silent, my determination to visit Schilthorn 007 the next day remained firm in my heart.

Annie shared the hotel confirmation of the next destination. By 5 pm, we arrived at Interlaken station, and en route to the hotel, Harder Kulm caught our attention. While walking, Annie inquired about the cost, and I said with the Swiss pass, it would be 17 francs, half the regular price. Upon reaching Harder Kulm, there was a long line, requiring at least 30 more minutes to get to the ticket counter. Peter expressed interest in visiting the next day to see the view, but I wasn't too excited about it. After 10 minutes, Peter grew impatient and suggested Annie check the ticket machine, similar to an ATM to skip the line. I quickly added, "Don't buy for me," knowing that the 50% Swiss pass discount can only be applied by human representative at the ticket counter, as common sense tells that an ATM wouldn't have provision to recognise a Swiss pass.

Annie informed Peter that the price was 34 Swiss francs. Peter instructed her not to make the purchase and stayed in the queue. Annie quietly asked me why I said not to buy your ticket but let them buy their tickets at a higher price. I explained I had already told them about the discount with the Swiss pass, and it only works if you show it to a person, not an ATM. Peter and Annie talked in their language, and I couldn't understand.

After few minutes, Peter expressed the desire to rest at the hotel, planning to explore Harder Kulm the next morning because he was tired. Annie suggested I proceed with the activity, and I agreed since I didn't want to mess up my plans to visit Schilthorn the following day. They left, and I stayed in line. When it was my turn to get on the tram, my phone battery was at 5%, worrying me about how to take photos of the stunning place. I prayed for a miracle, and luckily, a young couple stood next to me, the girl had a power bank with an Apple cable. Without hesitation, I showed them my phone with a 5% battery and requested for an 8-minute charge during the tram ride.

Tip: If your phone battery is almost empty and you'll need it later, avoid turning it off with the intention to switch it back on later. This can make the batter run out even faster and sometimes the phone won't turn on. Instead, putting it on airplane mode and leaving it on will use less battery.

They happily agreed, and when I got off, my battery was at 11%. I planned to catch the second-to-last tram at 8:40 PM, with the final tram leaving at 9:50 PM. I noticed a queue for solo pictures at a scenic spot. I looked around to find someone skilled in photography. After getting my pictures taken, I leisurely explored the area and opted to dine at one of the restaurants, savouring a delightful meal of Thai soup and bread.

The soup serving was generous enough for two people. After dinner, I returned to the tram point, intending to catch the 8:40 PM tram, only to discover a substantial queue with over an hour of waiting. Unable to board the 8:40 PM tram, I patiently waited in line for the next and final tram at 9:50 PM. It was already 9 PM, and with only 1% battery on my mobile, I texted Annie about the delay, opting to board the last tram. Peter replied, saying they were also out and would be delayed. Thankfully, my phone turned off after reading his message. I got back to the resort at 10:20 PM, and they weren't back yet. Placing my phone on charge, I went to the restroom. When Annie and Peter returned and didn't find me, they grew worried. Peter suggested, "We should go and check."

After I came out of the restroom, they expressed they got worried not seeing me.

I explained that my mobile had switched off, so I charged it and had to use the restroom urgently. Annie, brimming with excitement, shared that she visited the same hotel where we saw the corporate party and proudly displayed a Swiss watch, a gift from her husband. Seeing my friend so happy, I felt satisfied that Peter had finally listened to my suggestion of treating his wife to a candlelight dinner and giving her special gift. They retired to their room, and I began packing, knowing we had to check out in the morning.

Annie returned to ask about my plans for the next day. I shared that I intended to visit Schilthorn 007. Peter, who overheard from the other room, rushed in and loudly questioned, "How can you go to Schilthorn 007?"

I replied, "I'm going because it's one of the attractions I wanted to see."

Peter exclaimed, "We have a train to Zurich tomorrow; you can't go. I've shown you the Schilthorn area so we have covered it."

I didn't like someone raising voice at me, I replied, "It wasn't the 007 spot," and signaled to Annie that I would talk to her privately.

As Peter left grumbling, I whispered to Annie, "I can't speak in front of him but will tell you."

Annie remarked, "You can talk in front of him; he's not that bad."

I found Annie's statement odd because it's more comforting to have a woman-to-woman conversation who is a friend rather than talking to a friend's husband, where you can't speak freely. I sensed that Annie might have blurted our conversation about Peter causing stress to others and hindering enjoyment in flow of conversation during the excitement of being treated by her husband. It appears Peter might have brainwashed her against me. A real game changer on last day.

I responded, "I really want to do 007, and I can explain it to you, but I can't express it to him because he gets hyper about everything, and I don't want him to get anxious. Moreover, my dad loved 007 movies, so it feels like a tribute to him by visiting that place."

Annie acknowledged, "Yes, that's fine, and I understand. But we have to leave in the morning. How long will you take? We have to check out of this resort and check-into the hotel in Zurich."

I replied, "I'll leave early in the morning. I don't want to disrupt your plans, feel free to continue with your plans and I will do what I intend to see. It's the final part of the journey, and as I mentioned during the passport loss incident, I won't alter my itinerary. Besides, you have your passports to travel back now."

Peter, naturally eavesdropping, rushed in said loudly in a rude tone, "We apologize for disrupting your journey." Then, he slammed his hands together like namaste and in an unpleasant tone, "Thank you for being with us during our tough times."

This inappropriate gesture caught me off guard, and I told Annie, "My family thinks highly of you, and they have never said anything negative about you."

It was amusing to see that Peter found it hard to take compliments for his wife and remarked, "Nobody's perfect; everyone has flaws." This habit of downplaying his wife's praise was noticeable from the start of the trip.

At this point, I had run out of patience and firmly responded, "Yes, everyone has flaws, and I will make a list of yours and give it to you."

Annie turned her head from left to right like a shuttlecock between Peter and me, unsure of what to say.

I continued, "I don't even know if I have a hotel reservation in Zurich. Annie said it's not booked, and Peter claimed he sent confirmation. Both of you said different things. I don't even know who to believe. Now, I would have to make another reservation"

Annie questioned, "When did I mention that the hotel reservation hasn't been made?"

I replied, "During the train journey." Annie's statement gave me the impression that she might have spoken absentmindedly, possibly influenced by Peter scolding her for misplacing his credit card.

Tip: Group travellers should promptly share their reservation confirmations with each other instead of waiting until the last minute.

Annie responded, "I don't recall saying that, and I forwarded the hotel reservation in the evening today."

While I can empathize with Annie's emotional struggles during the trip, including the loss of her passport and her husband's behaviour, which may have caused her to be less attentive, I understand that she may have inadvertently informed me that the hotel booking was not done. I can relate to this because stress can affect one's ability to focus. However, I find it puzzling that Peter, who has always asked for confirmation of bookings made by me, waited until the second to last day of the trip to share the hotel booking made by him, especially considering that I had given him all the confirmation of reservations well before the trip.

I added, "That reservation doesn't even include the address."

Peter headed to his room, and I, displaying frustration, tossed one of my shirts onto the suitcase as I began packing. Turning to Annie, I remarked, "In a way, I'm sorry that an older person has to apologize to me. My upbringing isn't such that an elder should apologize."

Annie sat on the bed and expressed, "I had such a beautiful evening with my husband, and now the mood is completely spoiled. My husband is not a bad guy."

I mentioned "Nobody is bad; we're all good people. It's just a situation. This wouldn't have happened if you had asked about my plans. I planned to visit the 007 site, and you could have asked about our travel to Zurich. I would have suggested meeting at the train station. All you had to do was tell me the chosen train time, and the conversation would have concluded differently."

It struck me as odd that they discouraged me from going separately when I desired to visit 007, yet they were comfortable with the idea of going separately to visit the windmill and cheese factory in Amsterdam and decided to meet at a particular time. Similarly, when they chose to have dinner separately, they were okay with me visiting Harder Kulm. It appears that whether I accompany them or not depends on what suits their convenience.

Annie conveyed that "Peter hasn't decided on the departure time yet, as we'll be heading to Harder Kulm. How do you plan to check out"

I mentioned, "I'll check out in the morning and leave my bags at the reception. Can you provide the hotel's address?"

Annie responded, "The hotel booking has been forwarded, and you can find the address on Google."

I said "Then I request you to find and share it with me as sometimes there can be chain of hotels in city of same brand and I want to be sure of the address if I'm travelling alone, like you saw in Lucerne, we went in different directions because of multiple hotels of same brand. So, I'd rather get the address directly from you since you booked it."

On the last day, I wanted to avoid the risk of heading to the wrong address in a foreign land, hence my insistence on knowing the address.

Annie mentioned, "I have a question about the Harder Kulm ticket. You advised against buying your ticket but were fine with us purchasing a higher-priced one."

I responded, "I didn't stop you because Peter insisted you to buy Harder Kulm tickets. I had already informed you about half-price tickets of 17 euros. We were entitled for a discount with the Swiss pass, but if your husband insisted on buying at full price just to skip the line, I wasn't interested. I preferred saving my 1700 rupees discount by buying it at the counter."

I remembered how he complained to Annie in their language at the Colosseum because I bought the ticket at the regular price instead of 40-euro ticket he wanted to buy on the black market for a quick view. I wanted to avoid his complaints, so I directly told them they could go ahead and buy whichever ticket they preferred. I'm still confused about what bothered Peter. In Rome, he complaint that I didn't buy a 40-euro ticket from a scalper at the Colosseum, and at Harder Kulm, he secretly told Annie that I was fine with them paying more to skip the line. Sometimes, it makes me think maybe he doesn't want his wife to have smart friends because he feels insecure.

Annie mentioned, "When you talked about your family suggesting not to travel with someone's husband or brother again, you must tell your family that my husband was only being protective of you. You are misunderstanding him; he has lot of concern for you. He always checks if you've eaten, if you've returned or not, The other day, when you were alone at the breakfast table, he suggested that they join you, but I intervened, mentioning that you were on a personal call hence we sat on separate table"

It occurred to me that throughout the entire one-month trip, we always had breakfast separately. In shared accommodations, I would have breakfast first, allowing them space to get ready, and vice versa. In places where we had independent accommodations, I consistently arrived early and spent time taking pictures or talking on mobile. It was only in Venice that we ate together, and on some occasions, we packed food due to early train departures. In reality, we had eaten breakfast together only once. So, I didn't understand the relevance of giving me company on one day. I didn't voice these thoughts.

I replied, "Protective of what?" silently contemplating how to convey to this innocent lady what transpired at the Heineken Museum.

I wondered, if they were truly worried about my safety because below incidents do not demonstrate his protective nature:

- Taking a single girl to Red-light area and only revealed there that her husband wanted to visit Red-light area. Had it been disclosed at hotel I would have stayed at hotel.
- Why sent her husband to my room at 9 PM to get the Coke bottle, why she didn't come to pick in spite being on same floor and few rooms away.
- Near embassy Peter had put his hand on my waist and I screamed and you turned to look. Later you told me in room that we are modern people and there are no emotions in hug.
- Peter was drunk at Heineken Museum and had put his hand on my hip while you were ahead of us. He wanted to go to Lover's Canal and kept insisting that I accompany, he was even willing to pay for my ticket. I declined multiple times, & you didn't show any interest to stop your husband. Your husband scolds you if you ask for an extra drink and he even eats a snack without

offering you, do you think he will spend 16 euros on me.

- You asked why I sat far or separately from both of you in boat, trains, all the above are the reasons why I had kept distance from your husband.
- Peter asked me to book bus from France first even if it's late night in spite of my insistence that I will do it later. He forced me to book a non-refundable late-night bus, which I never boarded, I never expressed dissatisfaction that because of your husband I suffered loss of money.
- Why didn't you include me in their cab ride from their hotel to Antwerp Central station? They were aware that I would be walking alone to train station, especially since the night before, I had expressed fear and nervousness about potential encounters involving individuals of African descent.
- When the train to Switzerland was cancelled, Peter, after conversing with the representative, shared that only one ticket was available. He then suggested we use the Train app to book our tickets. This prompts the question of why he planned for Annie to be on one train while he and I travelled on another. A gentleman would have mentioned the limited availability of tickets and considered options for all passengers on the next train, at least this would have been my approach that all of us are on one train. This raises another question: Did he intentionally avoid taking my ticket to the reservation counter? I had informed Annie at the station that he didn't take my ticket? Was

he anticipating that he and I would be left behind to travel together?

- Lastly, when the representative re-issued the ticket, they informed me that Peter had specifically requested a business class ticket for both of you. The travel class itself is not a concern, but what left me disappointed was the self-proclaimed statement that "You had concerns for me." Peter could have easily called and proposed that both Annie and I sit together in one class, while he managed in another. This raises the question of where the genuine concern was in this situation.
- I perceived their selfishness when Peter refused me to use washing machine

I wanted to voice all the above and tell my friend that protection is not about asking someone if you have eaten. There's a significant distinction between verbalizing concern and protection and the actual actions taken. However, I decided not to say anything respecting the age of my friend.

In reality, I was the vigilant one ensuring their safety throughout the journey:

1. Cancelled my onward journey to support them during passport loss
2. When Annie's husband was inside the shop in Florence, I proposed that both of us should go inside upon observing hefty guy entering the shop.
3. Every time I noticed Peter showing money in public, I made a point to advice against it for safety reasons.

4. I recommended reaching out to the hotel to inquire about the jacket, in case it was accidentally left there.
5. Provided travel adapter and ensuring their devices are powered before me. I advised not to spend on buying another adapter
6. Introduced to the contact at embassy that gave them right direction
7. I advised Peter to check his emails to identify where the card was last used to contact and retrieve it accordingly
8. I suggested they should file a claim with their travel insurance, as it might offer recovery and potential compensation benefits
9. Peter had hidden the details of his return flight from Zurich, risking denial of boarding due to an EC (Emergency Certificate) issued by the embassy in the Netherlands. This would have led to a forced return to Amsterdam and incurred additional expenses for purchase of tickets. Thanks to my contact, they received right information and were able to save money. Additionally, got them discount on train tickets.
10. I consistently advised them to remain vigilant and keep a close eye on their bags near the train's baggage compartment.
11. Multiple times, I assisted in locating Peter's credit card or Annie's purse, which had been dropped on the bus.

12. During the passport loss incident, I ensured their comfort and assisted with the check-in process at hotels.

13. Despite the overnight journey (Rome) and hotel check-in process, Peter urged us not to rest and rushed us to sightseeing by depositing luggage with receptionist in destinations like Lucerne, and Venice. only to later complain about feeling fatigued due to low stamina.

While they may have felt they were protecting me, however, the above clearly indicates they were supported by me on every occasion. We missed doing many activities such as gondola rides, cycling in Amsterdam, visiting Lake Como, and exploring Vatican City. His excessive confidence wasted a lot of time in finding the direction to Lake Thun and Michelangelo's point

Annie responded, "The moment we entered and couldn't find you, he suggested, 'Let's go and find her. He was worried, we should have taken your mum number earlier so that we could have informed her.'

I replied, "But I had messaged earlier about the delay due to the last tram. I'm in mid-forties and I don't need protection, I'm not a small child that I can't manage myself, what will you tell my mum? I will be touching 50 in few years. Moreover, they know how exactly I travel"

It seemed they believed they should protect me because I'm a lady. But then, there was something not right – Eve teasing at Heineken or outside the embassy. Safety should begin with the person you're traveling with, shouldn't it? If there's teasing even from co-travellers, where's the safety in that? Something to ponder. I thought about expressing all this to her, but her husband treated her exceptionally well during the last part of the trip, and I didn't want to further ruin her good mood. Another reason for withholding my thoughts is that families often support each other, even when they're in the wrong.

Annie pointed out, "You call us old, but you'll be oldie also in the next few years."

I replied, "Certainly, but at that time, you'll be a senior citizen."

Annie added, "We've travelled domestic with another female traveller in her thirties before, and it was a pleasant trip. I understand that you're different, and we have different views."

I inquired, "Is it because of the food?"

Annie clarified, "No, it's not about the food. We noticed earlier that you like to buy your own meals. During our domestic travels with other couples, we used to contribute specific amount of money and cover all expenses from that pooled fund. However, you didn't follow this method on this trip."

I said "This is an international trip, I will pay for my food, sightseeing and shopping. Sharing will take place for cabs, hotels and public transportation. Whenever I travel internationally with friends or even on domestic trips, we each cover our own costs."

I further added "You explored Rome for me despite being tired and didn't want to see more sights, so you don't have to pay for the metro - I will cover that expense"

Annie said "No, it's not like that, every time you can't have an upper hand, earlier you treated with lunch, we are not the type to hold someone's money."

When Annie made a sarcastic comment at the metro station in Rome, saying she bought her metro tickets to join me in visiting the attractions despite her stamina, a usual response would be, "I'll cover the metro expenses," and that's what I had said at that time. However, after noticing my generosity, she might have playfully adjusted her statement to something like, "You can't have an upper hand……we are not the type to hold someone's money"

I nodded

Annie said "Can you check with your mom if her response would change, knowing our perspective that my husband was being protective of you and worried when he didn't see you in the room? You can take your time, maybe ask this question in 3 or 6 months."

I responded "Yes, sure"

In my heart I knew my mum's answer would still be the same bcos as a woman she understood but it seemed Annie chose to ignore these issues despite witnessing them firsthand.

Annie asked "What's the plan for tomorrow"

I replied "I'll check out in the morning and leave my luggage at the reception. You can text me the train timings you plan to catch, and if I can make it, I'll definitely text you and join you.

I continued with my packing and Annie left for her room.

A little later, she entered into the kitchen, in search of something, slamming cupboards in frustration. I could tell she was dealing with both her husband's frustration and a friend's venting in the last days of the trip. While she took in the frustration from both, but struggled to find a release for her own frustration, leading to her reaction with slamming the cupboards.

Prior to retiring for the night, I washed my green tea mug and left it to air dry on the kitchen counter. Although there were other unwashed utensils used by Annie and Peter, I opted not to clean theirs, as I believe in everyone taking care of their own responsibilities.

Tip: Before leaving the resort apartments, make sure to wash the dishes. If you notice any broken items when you check-in, take a picture and let the front desk know. This can prevent you from being charged extra.

In the morning, I woke up early and was able to get ready on time, thanks to resort for having a separate bathing area. After getting ready, I headed to the reception to drop off my luggage and returned the room keys. Carrying my Armani backpack, I packed only the essentials, which proved handy as I could easily rotate it to rest against my chest, alleviating any concerns about someone accessing the zipper of my bag and potentially loosing items.

Tip: When you're in a crowded place like a train, attraction, or bus, turn your backpack around so it rests against your chest. This prevents theft and gives you more room.

A staff member recommended catching the 7:20 AM train instead of the 8 AM to reach Schilthorn early, grab a window seat at the revolving restaurant, and enjoy a less crowded setting. Following their suggestion, I quickly went to the train station. I was happy to take their advice because it turned out to be a beautiful experience, reaching early and avoiding the crowds.

Tip: Taking tip from locals always helps.

Upon entering the train, I shared a seat with a young American couple of Indian origin. We had a delightful conversation, and I learned they were on a two-month Europe tour, a special anniversary gift from the husband to his wife before they planned to start a family. They wouldn't be traveling for the next two years once they start a family. The pleasant chat made the journey enjoyable, and we smoothly arrived at the station. A short walk from the station brought us to a bakery, where the bus awaited to take us to Schilthorn. After the driver grabbed his breakfast from the bakery, we headed to Schilthorn to board the cable car. Fifteen minutes later, the bus transported us to the cable car point. I took the lift to level 1. We needed to traverse five mountains, changing cable cars five times. The first three changes were free, and for the fourth one, a ticket was needed, but my Swiss pass granted a 50% discount. Upon reaching Schilthorn, it felt like our cable car was the very first to arrive at the restaurant. I swiftly captured a few of my own photos and assisted others by snapping their family pictures. Eventually, I found a window seat in the restaurant to enjoy a splendid view. Opting for the buffet, the meal was impressive, offering a range from vegetarian to non-vegetarian dishes, juices to alcoholic beverages, assorted soups, various breads, and even coffees adorned with a 007 design on the froth. The buffet choice allowed a leisurely seating of one and a half hours. I relished my buffet meal at Schilthorn.

I also contacted the hotel to ask if they could arrange a light breakfast for me since I missed the morning meal, something I could nibble on and use for lunch later. The receptionist acknowledged my request and said it would be ready for pick up when I collect my luggage.

When settling the bill for the buffet at the Schilthorn, the steward unexpectedly requested a tip, which struck me as unusual since in Switzerland, tipping is not customary as it is in the USA, where it's customary to leave at least 4% tip of the bill. Taking into account his senior citizen status and his request for a tip, I decided to leave a 4 euro tip by rounding off my 36 euro for buffet breakfast bill to 40 euros.

Tip: Verify if tipping is customary in the country you are visiting.

After a few hours, I hopped on the cable car to head back, then took a bus to reach the train station. During this time, I got a message from Annie stating that they were catching a train. What surprised me was that she texted me just 2 minutes before the train's departure, indicating a clear intention not to include me. Nonetheless, it didn't bother me, as my priority was covering the attractions I wanted to see.

On my way back, I snapped some lovely pictures of the waterfront and Kursaal Garden, including the Yash Chopra statue again. When I got back to the hotel, I picked up my bags, and the receptionist handed me the packed light breakfast, which included muffins and fruits.

Across from the hotel was a bus stop; however, after waiting for 20 minutes with no sign of the bus, I learned that a roadblock was causing delays or route changes. I decided to walk to the train station, which took me 15 minutes. I selected a direct train to avoid transfers, and the journey lasted 2 hours.

Counting the cities, you travel is a source of motivation.

Chapter 10

Embracing the Journey: From Endings to New Beginnings

Rhine Falls is popular tourist destination in Zurich, similar to Niagara Falls. However, on this Europe trip, I only had one night in Zurich. Since most international flights arrive in Zurich and travelling to Lucerne and Interlaken requires a separate plane or train journey, I had chosen to explore Lucerne and Interlaken first. I saved Rhine falls for future trips and decided to explore only the chocolate factory with limited time in hand.

Upon reaching Zurich, I checked the bus route to my hotel. Outside the train station, I saw three men of African descent on the path to the bus stop. Choosing a different route, I took a left and then a right, running parallel to the bus stop. Interestingly, there was a police van on this road, providing a sense of comfort.

When I reached the hotel, I finished the check-in process. The receptionist informed that Annie and Peter were out for a walk. I asked about the Lindt chocolate factory, inquiring about directions and closing time. The receptionist said it closes at 6 pm. Pressed for time, I quickly got ready, walked ten minutes to the bus stop, and took a 15-20-minute ride to the factory.

Tip: Travellers arriving via flight can choose to stay near airport. They have a free shuttle to take you to hotel

Tip: Explore hotel near train station that connects you to any station.

Upon arrival, the lady at the ticket counter told me that prior reservations were necessary, and all tickets were sold out. However, she suggested I explore the ground floor, look around, and enjoy the coffee shop. Although I missed out on the tantalizing tour of Swiss chocolate heritage, the place was still phenomenal. It was beautifully adorned, offering a delightful shopping experience with a variety of chocolates, ice creams, and souvenirs available for purchase. I bought some chocolates, savoured my coffee, snapped a few pictures for memories, bought few souvenirs and took the return bus.

Tip: Purchase an additional general souvenir gift that could be suitable for someone you might think of after returning from the trip.

After getting off the return bus, I walked back to the hotel. At the crossing, I bumped into Annie and Peter, exchanged greetings, and then headed back to my hotel room while they continued with their plans.

While preparing for departure the next day, I was occupied with packing my belongings in the evening. As I needed to show my shoes in the bag alongside other clothes, I employed a strategy to ensure that the shoe odour didn't affect the clothing as I couldn't find any plastic bag. I utilized hotel shower caps to wrap the smelly shoes before placing them in the suitcase, effectively preventing any unpleasant odours from spreading.

Tip: Using hotel shower caps to wrap the shoes before packing them in the suitcase, preventing any unpleasant odours.

Tip: Carry few poly bags in your suitcase or ask for laundry bag from the hotel.

In the evening, Annie came to my room and brought back a special item from Amsterdam that I forgot at the Interlaken hotel. I was grateful she brought it to Zurich, as it was something my mom specifically wanted. Annie asked about my day's activities, and I was excited to recount my experience at 007 Schilthorn, featuring an auditorium with various movies, an unlimited buffet, and alcohol. Annie mentioned, "Peter also loves James Bond movies; he would have enjoyed going there."

I doubted Annie's statement because the day before, Peter had claimed we already saw Schilthorn during our return from Jungfrau. Since he usually checks directions and costs before visiting attractions, his remark suggested disinterest in going back the next day. The cost for this particular location was approximately 100 Swiss francs per person, making it 200 Swiss francs for both of them, and I doubted he would be willing to spend that much on a meal atop the mountain. Hence, Annie's statement contradicted Peter's usual behavior.

Annie said she planned to leave for the airport the next day, with her flight an hour before mine. Given that we all had to go to the same airport, it made sense for us to travel together and save on costs. Nevertheless, I suggested departing a bit later for a noon flight instead of early morning. I asked her to consult with her husband about going little late.

In the morning, I got ready and headed to the reception, left my luggage, and enjoyed breakfast. Around that time, Annie messaged about wanting to leave early. As I was having breakfast, I was flexible with the timing. When they arrived, they settled at a different table and I continued my ritual of phone calls while having breakfast. After I finished eating, I collected my bags and returned the key to the receptionist and waited for them to get their bags to the reception.

Peter arranged a cab for the airport. The taxi driver estimated a 30-minute journey. During the ride, we noticed the driver took a right bridge instead of a left one. He promptly recognized the mistake and stopped the car. Presumably intending to reverse for the shorter route, before he could reverse the police arrived and began questioning. The driver claimed a technical fault, prompting the police to inspect and they checked the trunk and other components. This entire episode was causing a delay for us. Concerned, Peter asked the police if they could provide transportation in their police car to the airport, but they declined, advising us to book a cab before they left. The cab driver started the car shortly after the police departed, and we eventually reached the airport. While their flights had assigned check-in counters, mine did not. They proceeded to check-in their bags while I waited in a corner.

After they checked in their bags and got boarding cards, they rejoined me. Annie offered a hug, and I embraced her. She commented, "The trip wasn't too bad," and I smiled. Peter and I exchanged folded hands a namaskar-like gesture, signalling a mutual avoidance of conversation.

They departed for immigration clearance, and I headed to check-in with a different airline. Attempting to claim VAT for my Italian purchases, I was told by the custom officer that it should have been done before entering Switzerland. Customs informed me that, despite Switzerland having a Schengen visa, they are not part of the European Union, and thus, no VAT refund was possible. They advised that the claim should have been made at the Lucerne train border when coming from Italy. Disappointed, I proceeded to immigration clearance, indulged in coffee, snacks, and window shopping on my way to the boarding gate. I realised I still had some leftover coins, so I opted to put them to use instead of allowing them to sit unused for years until the next trip to the same destination. I purchased packets of cookies to enjoy with my family.

Leftover Currency Tips:

1. If you find yourself with leftover currency upon leaving a country, consider using it to buy yourself a coffee at the airport or purchasing one to give to a sweeper, giving a generous tip to a waiter or donate it in a donation box. Unused currency is likely to go waste once you return.
2. Exchange the leftover foreign money for a Starbucks gift card. It turns the foreign currency into your local currency at a good rate. This way, you won't waste the money when you return home.

As a regular traveller, I had the privilege of being among the first to board, following the business class passengers. The aircraft lacked an aerobridge, requiring us to board via a shuttle bus to reach its parking spot. This allowed me the opportunity to take unique photos on the aircraft stairs without any background distractions. I expressed gratitude to the fellow passenger who took my lovely pictures, and the crew humorously mentioned, 'It's because we held the plane for you.' It brought a sense of relief and excitement, leaving me with a smile.

As I settled into the cabin, mixed emotions intertwined. On one side, the thrill of a solo trip through Bruges, Antwerp, Zurich, and the mesmerizing landscapes of partial Interlaken left cherished memories. On the other, a sense of fulfilment stemmed from standing up for Annie when her husband unfairly blamed her, advocating for recognition of her valuable contributions to his family along with standing by a friend during their lost passport incident.

Despite these positive aspects, a hint of sadness lingered due to the absence of gratitude from Annie and her husband Peter. My contacts and efforts played a crucial role, saving them from a potential loss of 7.5 lakhs. This included savings on buying new air tickets, existing travel arrangements, discounts on train tickets, and securing a refund for a non-refundable hotel stay, ensuring they have travel adapter throughout the remaining of the trip and helping them recover misplaced items multiple times. This realisation transformed the trip beyond a physical journey into an emotional odyssey. They didn't appreciate how I helped them stay safe during train trips and hotel check-ins, using my passport for their smooth travel leading to heartbreaking realisation that our friendship had reached its breaking point. It also brought forth valuable lessons that I carried with me from the trip. Even though my friend's husband had a tendency to rush through attractions, blame others, impulsive by nature, avoid paid attractions and change plans a lot, there was room for better collaboration. Talking about our habits before the trip could have helped us find better solutions over self-cantered thinking like establishing meeting points at a central location after everyone had seen their respective attractions. These Anxious thoughts fluttered like butterflies and made me realise some important things for married women to consider from this trip:

1. Is it advisable to start with a local trip involving the solo traveller, friend, and her family to evaluate compatibility and tolerance levels before embarking on an international journey?

2. Should a married woman refrain from walking fast ahead of others, opting to walk alongside either the solo traveller or her husband to avoid causing discomfort for the solo traveller?

3. Shouldn't the travellers clearly communicate financial arrangements, as assumptions from previous trips may not automatically apply to new travellers.

4. Would it be beneficial to establish clear rules and expectations for the trip?

5. Married women should be careful not to burden their single friends by advising them to talk to their spouses when they call to speak with you. This might make their husbands more at ease with single women and attempt to assert dominance in the situation.

6. Married women need to strike a balance between their friends and family. If a married woman is aware of her husband's perspective, she should take the initiative to resolve the matter rather than waiting until the last three days of the trip.

Some lessons for solo travellers:

1. Family members will support their own people, even when they are wrong or behave inappropriately.
2. Choose friends or travellers who are also solo travellers for international trip
3. Traveling with friends' families could mean having to give up on preferred sightseeing since not everyone might be interested in the same things. It can feel tough if two family members team up, as the solo traveller might end up missing out on what they want to see.
4. If most of the travellers aren't from the same family, there won't be many changes to the plans.

These lessons might not apply to everyone, as everyone is unique, with varying levels of maturity and understanding. The story provides insights into the challenges one might face - whether you stand by someone in tough times or continue on your journey, whether you appreciate those who helped you or ignore them, and whether you contribute to an expensive meal that includes non-vegetarian options and alcohol while you stick to vegetarian choices. In the end, it's about the choices we make - whether they're good, bad, or ugly.

Excitement bubbled up like fizzy soda as the plane taxied down the runway, thinking about the happy reunion waiting at home. As the journey ends, we see how getting along with each other is super important when we travel across the Globe and leave the trails behind. If a wife knows her husband is a bit bossy, it can be okay because they understand each other. But when different people with their own ways of doing things travel together, it can get tricky. It gets even harder when people, trying to be polite and respectful, don't speak up about what they feel. Through the pages of this story, we've glimpsed into the varied hues of adventure and tested the waters of resilience. As we finish this adventure, remember that talking openly and treating everyone with respect makes our travel experiences better, like different colours making a beautiful picture.

Last Tip: May this travel book not just mark the end of a narrative but the beginning of new adventures inspired by the lessons shared. Travel isn't just about the destinations; it's a journey of self-discovery and connection. So, here's to embracing the unknown, navigating challenges, and creating stories that resonate long after the last chapter. Let every tip shared be a compass for your future explorations, and may your travels be filled with joy, growth, and the magic of discovering the world and yourself.

Once you've gone on a trip, it stays with you forever. Your thoughts are always traveling, even when you're not.

Back on Home Turf: Time to Plot Next Adventure!

Upon you return-

1. Review your bank and credit card statements meticulously to identify any possible fraudulent activity. It's a good security measure to check for any discrepancies, especially since you used your credit card at various merchant outlets.
2. Place important documents such as your passport and foreign currency back in their regular place where you typically store them. This is likely to be the first spot you'll look for them when preparing for your next trip.
3. Keep your packing list and incorporate any additional items you discovered during this trip to create the ultimate packing list for future endeavours.
4. Start mapping out your next dream destination
5. Meet your friends to share travel tales

After returning from my trip, I got settled and caught up with my friend Sophie to swap travel tales and give her the Armani purse. Our friendship is built on openness, so Sophie felt comfortable expressing that the purse wasn't quite her style. Drawing from my experience in customer service and knowing that major brands often accommodate exchanges, I reached out to Armani store to explore swapping the purse for something more suitable.

Despite my best efforts, the store in India declined to exchange the product due to their policy. Although my friend was fine with keeping it, I was determined to pursue better customer service. After contacting Armani's customer service via email, I was redirected to their European department since the purchase happened in Schengen country, which, regrettably, refused the exchange due to the elapsed 30-day period. Given the impracticality of traveling to Europe for this, I knew it was crucial to think strategically.

After exploring all avenues, I contacted Armani's head office in the USA, emphasizing that they could verify my loyalty as a customer through my earlier purchases. I proposed an exchange, offering to cover any price difference for a new item. Thankfully, the representative was understanding and liaised with the India store to facilitate the exchange. When Sophie and I arrived at the store and selected our outfits, there was a delay as the representative had to consult their manager for approval. Rather than waiting, we opted to grab coffee at Paul's and asked them to call and share the price of the product. Upon receiving the call about the product price, I felt disheartened to learn it was 6500 rupees, slightly lower than the original purchase price. Upon returning to the store and confirming with the representative, she clarified that the purse was priced at 11000 rupees. Additionally, she explained that the 6500 rupees was the difference in price between the purse and the two shirts we intended to buy. The higher exchange price compared to the original purchase price was due to the inclusion of 2000 rupees of GST. While I couldn't get a VAT refund at the Zurich airport for Armani, I was pleased that it was offset through the exchange. This experience reminded me that nothing is impossible until you try, even when faced with the word "Impossible," as it truly spells "I'm possible."

Tip: If you claim VAT, remember that you'll need to submit the original receipts to customs at the airport. This means you'd lose the opportunity to exchange any item later without the bill.

Choose your dream countries.

TRAVEL VIABILITY

How to ask for directions without looking like a tourist?

When you want to show someone a map for directions, go into a store and ask the shopkeeper for help. Instead of holding the map out in the open, put it in your purse. When you need to check the location's name, discreetly look into your purse like you're searching for something, quickly see the name, and then close the bag. Another option is to take out the map while you're inside a shop for a more subtle approach.

How can I give the impression that I'm part of a group instead of traveling alone?

If you come across a traveling group, consider sticking with them. When I was in Bruges, I noticed a tour guide taking awesome pictures of his group while we were waiting to get on the canal. I asked for a photo, and it turned out really nice. However, be careful before handing over your camera to strangers. The muggers travelling in groups can swiftly pass your phone among themselves. The tour guide recommended that, as a solo traveler, I must carry a stick and asked to join their group to enjoy some attractions together.

How do you decide who to hand your phone to for taking pictures?

1. I usually give my camera or phone to people with kids. Sometimes, I ask young girls if they can take my picture. In Antwerp, I saw a group of five girls eating pizza on the street. I felt safe asking one of them,

figuring the ones busy with their food wouldn't leave it to run away with my camera.

2. Once, at Lover's Bridge in Bruges, I gave my camera to some young girls. One of them, a bit on the heavier side, also asked for my jacket and small bag with things like snacks, water, and souvenirs. While it made me a bit nervous to hand over my belongings, the constant flow of people on the small bridge reduced the likelihood of any untoward incidents.
3. I also request Indian women to take a photo, considering the "Brotherhood in a foreign land" logic, feeling a sense of unity.

What places should I stay away from to reduce the chance of running into thieves?

Don't stand near an open staircase at the train station. If your earbuds drop, you might have to choose between losing them or missing the train. Also, it gives a chance to thieves to toss something onto the staircase. This allows an accomplice to quickly grab it and make a fast escape.

Soak in experiences

General Tips

1. Check if the hotel room has window latches.
2. Travel on weekends for a 50% discount on train tickets to Brugge via Belgiumtrains.com. Couples enjoy a 1 plus 1 free offer.
3. Swiss pass holders receive discounts when inquiring at the ticket counter and ask for a discount.
4. Groups enjoy cheaper family tickets, and students benefit from reduced prices.

Remember that it's okay to be a tourist, and safety should always be a priority. It's more important to enjoy your travels and experience the local culture than to worry too much about fitting in perfectly.

How can you prevent others from identifying you as a tourist?

1. Dress like a local: Learn about how locals dress and try to dress the same way. Don't wear obvious tourist attire like fanny packs or clothes with big logos.
2. Use public transportation confidently: Familiarize yourself with the local transit system so you can navigate it without looking lost.
3. Walk with you know where you're going: Look confident and determined when you walk, even if you're unsure. Try not to use maps or guidebooks while walking around.

4. Learn basic local phrases: Knowing a few essential phrases in the local language can go a long way in making you seem less like a tourist.
5. Stay Alert: Pay attention to what's happening around you so that don't look lost or confused.
6. Avoid overusing your camera: While it's great to capture memories, constantly taking photos can label you as a tourist. Take pictures discreetly and respectfully.
7. Seek directions politely: If you're lost, ask locals for help in a friendly manner, as if you're just double-checking even though you know the area.
8. Avoid flashy displays of wealth: Keep valuable items out of sight, refrain from showing money in public and avoid displaying expensive jewellery or gadgets.
9. Learn about local customs: Knowing and respecting local customs and manners can help you fit in better.
10. Be mindful of your behaviour: Act respectfully toward the local culture and customs, and avoid behaviours that might draw attention.
11. Avoid carrying Selfie Sticks: These can clearly mark you as a tourist and draw unwanted attention.
12. Avoid Tourists waist pouches: The are designed for convenience and security but are often associated with tourists and can make you stand out in a crowd.

13. Avoid discussions of schedule in public: it's wise to limit discussions of your destinations and schedule with travel buddies that could be overheard by others, as it can be inadvertently reveal your status as tourists and attract unwanted attention.

Aim for Stars

Appendix

HELP

Helpful Numbers to be handy, both Toll free and Non Toll free

Ambulance	
Police	
International Operator assistance to call through calling cards or Collect Calls	
Embassy Details of the Country visiting: Phone numbers/ Address/ Email or website	
If using your mobile to call international then dial as you would dial in your own country to any international number.	

To dial local within the same country – Omit the country code	
To dial international by using a local number of the country you are visiting then prefix '00' before the country code.	
Credit Card or Financial Institutions Numbers	
Note Credit Card numbers in case of loss	
Travel Agent Number, in case change in ticket is required for a ticket booked through Travel Agent	
Useful Contacts of Family or Friends overseas	
Holidays and Festivals Dates	
Daily Itinerary	
Validity of passport should be 6 months else it requires a renewal	

Inform Financial institutions about your upcoming travel Check on the transaction fee	
Hotel Room Confirmation or Reference Number Phone Number Address	
Travel Insurance	
EuRail or Train Reservation	
Car Rentals with GPS	

All the above information will be useful when planning the itinerary and auto remind you if missed a thing.

Travel is the ultimate inspiration

About the Author

This book is an exquisite unveiling of horizons, demystifying the essentials of globetrotting with a wonderful account of first-hand experiences by the vivacious girl Nanzie. Like Alice and her quest of wonder land, Nanzie was fuelled with passion for airline industry, determined to be associated with aviation fraternity. She has worked with premium airlines; it was her unique opportunity to work with sales and passenger handling – the culmination of early years of her dream of travel across the seven seas and continents. Her foray into international travel was at a greenhorn age of 24 years, it was like riding a bike without training wheels. She was as nervous as anyone would be during their first trip abroad. However, it was packing like a backpacker and go crafted a new adventure that gave her the strength. She deems money weighs less than courage when it comes to traveling. She has extensive experience of travelling overseas both for leisure and business. Now she offers suggestion and recommendations to various travellers in her circle of friends. Various first-time travellers have consulted her and benefited from the proposals. She has headed large teams at companies to develop effective travel and logistics arrangement skills to the global enterprise. Passion for the airline industry and traveling to explore the other side of the world inspired her to share her real time travel experience with the world. She shares that intrepid travelling requires well-equipped strategies and exit plan. It is a reminder to all non-travellers to explore this world at their own unique pace and to all frequent travellers of facts previously unknown to them, opening new horizons with the confidence of travel security. This book has been written with masterly finesse of an autonomous traveller.

Recently someone asked Nanzie – "Why do you travel? What is your story?"

To the others astonishment Nanzie's response was "Travelling is therapeutic, adventurous and enchanting to unfold the unseen beauty of the world. I travel because it breathes a new air"

Good Luck and Happy Flying

Tips to start packing for your flight:

Safety Measures

1. After the COVID era, it's prudent to check the health status of the city you plan to visit.
2. Take safety measures and necessary precautions and any pre-tests or reports required prior to travel to avoid denied boarding at home country or immigration clearance at destination country

Purse

1. Always keep a pen in your hand luggage. It will be handy for filling out forms during immigration in your home country or for forms provided by crew members inside the aircraft for immigration clearance.
2. Choose a low-cost wallet over a branded one. Stash a small amount of euros in it. If you're ever robbed, surrender that wallet.

Various Currency Options

1. Travellers Cheque
2. Don't carry more than 200 euros or usd
3. Forex multi-currency card. You can reload through credit card anytime.

Money

1. Split your money or credit cards into four equal portions and spread them out in different locations.

Keep some cash in your wallet, some in your jeans, a few notes in your handbag or travel bag, and hide some in your socks or shoes. Also, put some in an envelope and staple it with your itinerary (as paper documents are less likely to be targeted for theft). This way, if you are robbed or lose any of these, you still have money stored in other spots.

2. Concealing cash is simple; just roll it up inside a lip balm container.

3. Take an empty body butter box or deodorant container and fill it with a credit card and some cash. Your money and cards will remain safe, as no one would think of looking at cosmetic containers.

4. Visit a tailor and ask for a cloth pocket with a zipper to be added inside your jeans, providing a secure hiding spot for your passport and valuable cards during your travels, thus ensuring their safety.

Essential documents packing

1. Always remember to carry a photocopy of your passport with you, either by emailing yourself a picture or scan copy. This can be invaluable in case you misplace your passport.

2. Store copies of essential documents such as passport and travel insurance, etc., in a secure location such as the icloud, email, or CamScanner. If you happen to lose everything, you'll be glad to have them accessible.

3. Prior to international travel, it's essential to create an itinerary using Excel or Word. This should feature

contact information for hotels, reservation details, emergency airline contacts for cancellations, phone number and address of your country's embassy in the destination country.

4. Keep a printed copy of your itinerary with you, and share another copy with your family so they are informed about your travel plans.

Hand luggage

1. Pack one or two extra outfits, along with socks, undershirts/bras, and underwear in your hand luggage. In case your luggage goes missing, you'll have a fresh set of clothes for after your journey or flight.
2. Prepare two pouches of medications and store them in both your check-in and hand bags. If one set of medication goes missing, you'll still have another set available as a backup.
3. Carrying your medication prescription can be helpful in purchasing replacements if you lose yours while traveling.

Check-in Luggage

To keep the shape of bras intact while packing them in a suitcase, you can:

1. Fill the cups with socks or underwear to help maintain their form.
2. Layering bras flat on top of each other, alternating the direction of the cups to prevent them from getting crushed.

3. Position bras in the middle of your suitcase surrounded by softer items like clothing to provide cushioning.
4. Avoid folding bras in half to prevent creasing and misshaping.

Others

1. Carry a hand towel. They're easy to fold, dry rapidly, and conveniently fit into a suitcase without adding any extra weight.
2. Don't forget to pack your bedtime attire at the bottom of your luggage. This makes sure that when you get to where you're going, you won't have to search through your whole suitcase to get ready for bed.
3. If you think you'll need a certain number of socks, add half of that amount to make sure you have enough.
4. Include travel-sized laundry detergent, such as Wheel and Tide sachets, in your packing to wash clothes by hand or use with an in-house washing machine at Airbnb accommodations.
5. Take with you a collapsible bag that won't take up a lot of room in your suitcase. It's helpful for carrying water bottles or storing items you buy while sightseeing. Additionally, it can be handy if you're overpacked and entitled to check in extra luggage.
6. Make sure to put a label with your contact details inside your luggage. Sometimes, security may check your bag randomly, and if the luggage tags on the outside fall off or are taken off while on the luggage

belt, the airline will look inside to find your contact information to identify the owner.

7. To make sure your luggage is easy to recognize, put a label on the outside and write your name and contact details on it.

8. Before you leave your bags at the baggage drop counter, snap a quick photo of your luggage. If your bag goes missing, showing the picture can help expedite the paperwork by giving an accurate description of your bag.

Medicine

Remember to carry a first aid kit equipped with essentials such as pain killers for stomach relief, medication for headaches, fever, diarrhoea, throat and a variety of bandages.

Electronics

1. Keep in mind the electrical outlets used in the country you're visiting. Purchase the right power adapter before you travel. It's more cost-effective to do so in your own country rather than paying seven times more in a foreign land.

2. Your travel electronics case should have your phone, earplugs, phone charger, a small pin (which usually comes with an iPhone box) to switch SIM cards from national to international, an extension cable, and a power bank for your devices. It can be hard to find free power outlets in public areas.

3. Jot down the serial numbers of all your electronics, such as your laptop, iPad, camera, and any others you have. Having this information will help the police return your stolen items to you more easily.

Carry travel weight scale

1. Always carry a travel light weight scale; it aids in checking the weight beforehand to avoid airport check-in hassles.

Important to get few things in order:

1. Consider applying for credit cards that offer points upon application or provide complimentary lounge access. Just ensure you maintain a good CIBIL score and pay off your credit card balance on time.
2. Explore the exchange rates offered in the country you plan to visit. At times, it can be less expensive to buy currency at your bank before you go.
3. Take a few extra passport photos with you when you travel. In emergencies, you don't want to search for a photo shop in a foreign country and end up paying 4 times more.
4. Explore your credit card benefits before departing, as the Regalia credit card, for instance, provides complimentary airport lounge access. You might have access to these facilities without knowing about them

NOTES

www.ingramcontent.com/pod-product-compliance
Lightning Source LLC
La Vergne TN
LVHW041158150826
845673LV00001B/211